D0436515

WHITE CAPTIVES

WHITE CAPTIVES

Evelyn Sibley Lampman

A Margaret K. McElderry Book

Atheneum   1975   New York

Library of Congress Cataloging in Publication Data

Lampman, Evelyn Sibley.
White captives.

"A Margaret K. McElderry book."
SUMMARY: A fictionalized account of the experiences
of two sisters who spent five years as Indian captives
in the mid-nineteenth century.

1. Oatman, Olive Ann—Juvenile fiction. [1. Oatman,
Olive Ann—Fiction. 2. Indians of North America—
Captivities—Fiction]
I. Title. PZ7.L185Whi (   ) [Fic] (   ) 74–18187
ISBN 0–689–50023–8

Published simultaneously in Canada by
McClelland & Stewart, Ltd.
Manufactured in the United States of America.
Printed by Sentry Press, New York
Bound by The Book Press, Inc.
Brattleboro, Vermont
Designed by Nora Sheehan
First Edition

*With much love for
the two finest young men I know
(in alphabetical order),
Jack Knutson and Jack McIsaac*

WHITE CAPTIVES

Chapter 1

THE SOUP TASTES FUNNY," SAID MARY ANN. She spoke under her breath so that her mother, on the other side of the campfire, could not overhear.

"It needs salt," whispered Olive. "Beans don't have much taste without lots of salt."

"It's just as nourishing this way," Lucy, their elder sister, told them reprovingly. "We have to make our salt last until we reach Fort Yuma. You should be thankful that you have something hot to put in your stomachs. We have a long night's travel ahead of us."

3

"Oh, we are," Olive said quickly. She dipped her slab of dry bread into the thin bean soup and bit off the soggy end. But Mary Ann was right. It did taste funny, a little like biting into flour and water paste.

"The moon's coming up. We'll be able to start before long," announced their brother, Lorenzo. He was fifteen, the eldest boy in the family, and was expected to do a man's work.

Olive sometimes thought that if it hadn't been for Lorenzo, Pa might not have been so determined to leave the Pima village on the mouth of the Gila River and strike out alone across Indian country. The Wilders and the Kelleys, the last two families to accompany the Oatmans that far, had been unwilling to leave the security of the friendly Pima Indians. But the Wilders and the Kelleys had no almost grown-up sons to share a man's work. Royce Oatman had. Besides he was stubborn. When Pa made up his mind to do something, he did it.

So much had happened since Pa began carrying out his latest scheme that Olive had trouble remembering it all. She wished she could have kept a diary, but it would have taken stacks of paper to hold it. And who could carry that much surplus weight in a covered wagon? Now, after seven months, she could only remember the highlights, not the little details.

It had begun on the day that Pa had come home

4

to their little farmhouse in Illinois and announced that they were moving west. Ma might have known before, but the children were given no advance notice. It was enough to take a body's breath away to hear that he had sold everything they owned and with the $1,500 had purchased an outfit for the trip.

Nobody had said anything against it, but Lucy, in particular, had not wanted to leave. Olive had caught her crying in the barn and guessed the reason, but Lucy would never admit it. Lucy was seventeen, and there was a young man who had walked her home twice from Sunday services. But Lucy was a good girl and a devoted daughter. She kept reminding Olive over and over how hard the Illinois winters had been on Pa's back ever since he strained it lifting stones to build a neighbor's well. The winters in New Mexico, where they were going, were said to be mild, and there would be no more mornings when Pa ached so badly he could hardly get out of bed. Lucy insisted that she would be glad to go any place where Pa would be without pain.

Besides, Mormons were no longer welcome in Illinois. Three years before, a large party headed by Brother Brigham Young had left to found a splendid city in Utah Territory where they would be free from persecution. Pa had decided not to go at that time. Olive didn't know why, but she suspected that Ma had something to do with it.

There had been whispers about some of the apostles taking spiritual wives in addition to the wife they already had. Ma would have no dealings with that, and she had her ways of getting around Pa. They had stayed behind, but the Gentiles—as the people who were not Mormons were called—didn't forget easily that the Oatmans were Mormons. The little things, the slights and slurs, continued, so now they were headed west, only not to the new city on the great lake of salt but to build a New Zion and make converts. The Church of the Latter Day Saints approved of missionaries to spread the Mormon cause.

To tell about the August day in 1850 when they set out would have taken a lot of pages in Olive's diary if she had kept one. That day the white-topped wagons left Independence, Missouri, which Pa said was a wicked city. He had been glad they were camped well out of town so the innocent eyes of his seven children would not be contaminated by it.

There were fifty men, women, and children in their train, and the plan was to build their New Zion on the banks of the lower Colorado River in New Mexico. Olive had never been good in geography, but she knew it was some place far west and south. How excited everyone had been that day and how happy! It was like a great picnic on wheels—only the happiness did not last.

Almost immediately, the company began to

quarrel, and some of the mothers and fathers wouldn't speak to other mothers and fathers, which made it hard on the children, because they, too, had to ignore each other. They saw occasional bands of Indians, and once the men temporarily forgot their differences and took up guns to drive the savages away. But by the time they reached the Santa Fe Pass, tempers had grown so short that the party divided. Over half of them took the trail through Utah to join Brother Brigham Young in his fine city. The other eight wagons, led by Royce Oatman, traveled south to Socorro on the Rio Grande.

Olive was proud that her father had been elected leader of the group. His selection was not because he had made the trip before, but because he had been a schoolmaster and could read a map. He could even speak a little Spanish, having studied it when he was younger. People said Spanish would be useful where they were going, since Mexicans and many Indians spoke that language. But Olive did wish they hadn't run into so much trouble on their travels because people blamed Pa. It wasn't his fault that their food ran low and had to be replenished by hunting. Nor was he to blame when Apaches ran off most of their cattle one night.

They stopped at little Mexican settlements for provisions and repairs—Tubac, Santa Cruz, Tucson—and by ones and twos the owners of the wagons decided to stop, rather than risk the danger of an attack by the warlike Apaches. At the last stop, the Pima village, the Wilders and Kelleys had announced that there was safety in numbers and they would stay until a passing troop of cavalry could provide protection.

Pa had done his best to dissuade them. He argued late into the night, and Olive had fallen asleep listening to his voice giving argument after argument. The Pimas might not always be so successful in keeping the Apaches at a distance. What if they were overwhelmed? Originally, the Pimas had been farmers, but because of constant hostilities they had been forced to leave their gardens unattended and now were nearly destitute. Starvation was very close. It would be better to take a chance in the open country. The Apaches were old enemies of the Mexicans and the Pimas, but now this country belonged to America. The Apaches had no reason to quarrel with the Americans. Besides, Pa had known lots of Indians in the East. He knew how to deal with them. They were just like children and only took understanding.

It had done no good, and in the morning the Oatman wagon was the only one to roll out of the Pima village. Lorenzo marked the date on a little homemade calendar. It was March 11, 1851.

There was no question but that Pa was stubborn, Olive decided. She peered around Lucy to where he was sitting on the ground, silently dipping his share of dry bread into the cooling soup. And maybe now, a week later, he regretted his decision to continue on alone, two adults and seven children, across this wild country. Last night, when the team had bogged down on that little island midstream of the Gila River, Pa had covered his face with his hands and said, "Oh, Mother, I have a feeling there's even more trouble ahead." That was as close as he would ever come to admitting he might have been wrong.

"I can't eat it," said Mary Ann, pushing aside her bowl of soup. "It doesn't taste good."

"I'll eat it," volunteered Royce junior quickly. He was ten and always hungry. "I've finished mine."

"Mary Ann must eat her own soup," said Ma firmly. "Of all you children, Mary Ann has always been the frailest. It's because she's so picky with her vittles. She doesn't eat enough to keep a bird alive. Look at her. Anybody would think she was only five instead of seven years old."

Mary Ann made a little face, but she obediently dipped her bread into the soup and took a small bite. Olive watched her hungrily. Her own portion was already gone, but as Ma always said, Olive wasn't a finicky eater. Probably that's why she had grown large and husky and looked older than twelve.

"Can I have some more?" asked Royce junior. "These are awful little bowls, and there's still soup in the pot."

Ma shook her head. "We'll save the rest for breakfast. After you've traveled all night, you'll be hungry." With a bit of bread she mopped up the soup around the edges of the bowl and popped it into the mouth of the baby on her lap.

"I'm hungry now," muttered Royce junior, but he didn't say it very loud, and everyone pretended not to hear.

"Why are we going now?" asked four-year-old C. A. "Nighttime is when everybody's supposed to go to bed."

"The sun is hot in the daytime." Lucy explained more patiently than Olive would have done. C. A. had been repeating that same question over and over and still couldn't seem to understand. "Our poor cows and oxen are tired. It will be easier for them to travel after dark when it's cool."

"I liked it better the way it was before," insisted C. A. "Nighttime is to sleep."

"It won't make any difference to you," said Royce junior. "You'll sleep in the wagon anyway while the rest of us walk."

"We'd best get loaded up." Pa stood up, and Mary Ann and C. A., who were still lingering over their bowls, began chewing more rapidly.

10

"The moon will clear the mountains any minute, and then we'll have plenty of light. Lorenzo, bring up the teams, and I'll do the yoking. Royce, help your brother. Lucy, you and Olive hand things to your mother to pack in the wagon. Mary Ann, sit on that big rock over there so you can hold the rope for the lead team when the boys bring it around. C.A., you stay out from underfoot."

"C. A. can watch the baby," said Ma, with a smile. "It will be a help not to have him underfoot when I'm packing. See that he doesn't toddle off, C. A."

As she helped gather up the remains of the meal, Olive glanced around a little apprehensively. Everything looked different in the light of the full moon that now seemed to be balancing itself on the very top of the mountains. In the daytime, the country had been similar to all those weary stretches they had been crossing for the past week, but now it seemed a little frightening.

Just behind her was the Gila River. What had been a rather muddy stream was now turned to silver in the few places visible between the straggling brush on the bank. She couldn't remember that the current had been audible by day, but now it seemed to have gained a voice, a low, sinister chuckle. Mountain ranges rose east and north, black silhouettes against the starry sky, and to the south was wild uninhabitable tableland. The moon was not yet high enough to pick out details, but even in sunlight the south was a frightening place. The flat-topped bluffs, which gathered purple shadows in the afternoon, varied in size from giants to smaller slopes, and they were separated by deep gorges, with only occasional scrub brush for vegetation. Straight ahead stretched the dusty, stony trail that they must travel west. Olive wondered what they would find at the end.

"Olive, take hold of the featherbed," said Lucy's voice in her ear. "You know I can't lift it alone, and Ma's waiting to put it in the wagon first."

"Sorry," said Olive automatically, and hurried to take one side of the mattress filled with goose feathers that was her mother's prized possession.

It was the third time in twenty-four hours they had repacked the wagon, she thought resentfully. Whenever they came to a hill of any size, the two yokes of cows and one of oxen halted stubbornly. They now refused to pull a load uphill, and everything had to be taken out and carried by the Oatmans themselves to the top.

"We're just as tired as you are," Olive told the team that was being yoked into place. "And we walked just as far, too."

"Look!" Lorenzo's voice carried an unusual note of shrillness. "Look, coming down the road. Injuns!"

Olive whirled to stare over her shoulder. Lorenzo was right. Advancing down the stony road from the west was a group of Indians. They were too far away for her to distinguish them clearly, but there seemed to be a great number of them.

"They must be Apaches," said Lorenzo. "Shall I get the gun?"

For a moment Pa didn't answer, and in the moonlight Olive saw his Adam's apple move up and down above his collar.

"No," he said finally. "No gun. There's nothing to fear. Everybody go on with what you're doing. I'll talk with them."

Was Pa afraid of those Indians, Olive asked herself. She and Lorenzo, who had discussed the subject once when they were gathering wood for a fire, had agreed that Pa had been acting strangely ever since they left the Pima village. Usually so calm and sure of himself, he had become nervous and undecided. He even let Ma make some of the decisions. But he was brave now, she decided. She herself would never have been able to walk down the road to meet those painted savages.

As they drew nearer, she was surprised to see that they weren't painted at all, not the way the books always said. Their faces were dirty, but you couldn't count that. They stood erect, and their black hair hung loose over the shoulders of their fringed leather jackets. The jackets were long enough to come down over their hips, and since the brown legs below were bare, Olive decided scornfully that they didn't wear trousers. That was the mark of the savage. Any civilized man would have the decency to cover his legs. But at least they had shoes or rather moccasins made of leather, which looked quite comfortable. She was a little jealous of those moccasins, since her own shoes were beginning to pinch a trifle.

Pa spoke to the Indians, then he motioned them to stay where they were while he returned to the wagon.

"Un momento," he called over his shoulder.

"That's Spanish," Olive whispered to Lucy proudly. "Aren't we lucky that Pa knows Spanish so he can talk to the savages? He probably told them to keep their distance."

"But they're not doing it," said Lucy fearfully. "They're not minding him at all."

She was right. The Indians were trailing Pa to the wagon, their black eyes turning this way and that as they absorbed every detail.

"Get me that can of tobacco and the pipe," shouted Pa. "Quick! They want to smoke."

Once again Olive admired her father's farsightedness. Mr. Oatman did not smoke, since his religion frowned upon the use of tobacco, but before leaving he had laid in a supply and also a pipe, especially for emergencies like this.

"Indians always smoke peace pipes in friendship," he had informed his startled family in Illinois as he unwrapped his purchase and stowed it in the wagon. "It would be bad manners to refuse, and the tobacco might make a handsome gift for an Indian chief some day."

And now his words were about to come true. Olive watched while Ma tossed down the tin of tobacco and the pipe from the open end of the wagon. Pa caught them and turned, smiling, to rejoin his guests. Olive could tell by his expression that he was not too pleased to find they had followed him to the wagon.

Pa and the Indians—Olive counted, and there were nineteen of them—sat on the ground beside the dying fire. Pa filled the pipe, lit it from a coal, took a gingerly puff, and passed it to the man next to him.

"You Apache?" he asked self-consciously. Then he remembered and rephrased his question. *"Esta usted Apache?"*

The Indians nodded. "Apache," one agreed. Then, after a moment, "Tonto Apache."

Pa made a few more remarks while the pipe went around the circle, but since everything was said in Spanish, Olive could not follow the conversation. She felt very uncomfortable, for one of the Apaches kept looking at her, as though wondering what she was doing. And she wasn't doing anything at all. By now the wagon was

15

loaded, the team yoked into place, and they were ready to leave as soon as their unwelcome guests were on their way.

Suddenly Pa raised his voice and called out in English.

"Lorenzo, get some bread from your mother. We'll have to feed them before they'll go."

"Royce, we can't spare it!" Ma must have been listening, for now her head appeared in the opening behind the driver's seat. "You said yourself it's ninety miles to Fort Yuma. You'd be taking food from your children's mouths. Do you want them to starve?"

"Get the bread, Lorenzo," ordered Pa again, as though he hadn't heard.

Ma hesitated, then her face disappeared, and a few seconds later a loaf of homemade bread came sailing through the opening. As Lorenzo picked it up, Olive remembered that it was their last loaf and there was only enough flour for one more baking.

One loaf of bread divided among nineteen hungry Indians took no time at all to disappear. Although she could not understand their words, Olive could tell by their actions that they were demanding more. She could understand her father's actions, too. He was explaining that there was no more bread, telling the Indians how short the family was on food and urging them to take the can of tobacco instead.

Obviously, the Apaches did not want tobacco.

16

They retreated a few steps to gather in a cluster and discuss matters in their own language.

"I think we'd better leave," said Pa. "I've explained things to them as best I can. Mary Ann, give me that rope. C. A., you and the baby get into the wagon. Lorenzo—"

But whatever he was about to tell Lorenzo remained unsaid. Without warning, there came a deafening yell from behind. Olive, who had been reaching for the baby to lift him into the wagon, let her hands drop. At the same instant she felt herself being grasped by strong arms in fringed leather and carried to one side. She was thrown to the ground with such force that her breath was taken away.

All around her were sounds of violence, yells and screams, the lowing of frightened livestock, punctuated by something that sounded like thudding blows. She shook her head to get rid of the dizziness, and when she could focus her eyes, she was staring at something straight out of a nightmare.

Her father lay on the ground beside the lead team, moaning pitifully. Next to him was Lorenzo, with his face in the dust and the back of his head covered with blood. Even as she tried to struggle to her feet, Olive saw an Apache raise a war club high above his head and strike down her mother, who had leaped from the wagon in a futile attempt to rescue her baby.

The shock was too much. For the first time in her normal, healthy life, Olive Oatman fainted. When she regained consciousness, the yelling and moaning had stopped. Mary Ann was standing beside her, crying.

"Oh, Olive," she said between sobs. "Ma and Pa are dead, and all our brothers and sisters, too."

Chapter 2

TOAQUIN SAT ON THE GROUND BEFORE HER father's wickiup, pounding seeds in a stone *metate*. She was careful to keep her knees doubled to one side, with her heels partially concealed by her leather skirt, since that was the correct way for an Apache woman to sit. Now that Toaquin had seen eleven summers, she was an almost-woman and must begin thinking of such matters.

Her little sister, Wide Face, sat beside her, but since Wide Face was only eight, she was not so careful. Her legs were extended straight ahead, and she kept bumping her moccasined feet together in a most irritating manner.

"Do you think the raiding party will return soon?" asked Wide Face earnestly. "They have been gone a long time."

"It depends on how far they have to go," Toaquin told her, glaring at the bumping moccasins. "But Bad Heart will not return until he has avenged our people. Even if he must travel to the foot of the sky, he will find some *pinda lickoyi* and make them pay."

"They may not be the same *pinda lickoyi*—who killed our women and carried off our sister, Flowering Cactus, and the new wife of Bad Heart," argued Wide Face.

"What does that matter?" Toaquin frowned. Wide Face was such a baby. She would understand these things eventually, but sometimes Toaquin thought her little sister was slow in her mind. "A *pinda lickoyi* is any white eye. They are all enemies of the Apache."

Wide Face sat silently thinking about this, and Toaquin's arm moved up and down, crushing seeds with the stone.

All around them were the late afternoon sounds of the *rancheria*. Because the cold was lingering late this year, Angry Hawk's band of Tonto Apaches was still wintering in the sheltering draw along the edge of the desert, which sloped gently

20

o the Little Colorado River. Thatched wickiups made of willows were clustered in a semicircle below the face of the cliff, and cooking fires were now being built up by some of the women. Other women were carrying on with their regular endless tasks. Some were sewing on clothes, their bone needles piercing the tough skins to draw the leather or sinew thread through the openings. A party rounded the bluff, their backs bent under loads of firewood they had laboriously gathered, stick by stick. Two young girls carried pottery jars filled with rainwater left in crevices of the rocks. Old women bent their wrinkled faces above half-finished baskets, weaving them with the skill that comes only with years of practice. Most of the girls, like Toaquin, pounded seeds in stone *metates* for tonight's meal.

Small children under ten had no assigned tasks, and they played at their games—shinny or spinning tops. They were noisy, and their shouts echoing against the cliff made a great din, which caused their mothers to smile tolerantly. If there were need for silence, these same boisterous children knew how to breathe so gently that not even a stalk of grama grass would quiver. Here, however, in the wintering place that the Smart One, Angry Hawk, had chosen for his people, there was no need for quiet. Let the young enjoy themselves.

In the last splash of sunshine, soon to be gobbled up by the cliff, the men had gathered to talk together. At the moment their hands were idle, but that was as it should be. Men's work was harder and more dangerous than the work of women. No one resented that it left occasional time for relaxation. A man must go to war. He must guard the safety and the health of his family. When game was needed, it was the man who became the hunter, who killed and skinned and butchered, transporting the meat and hides over long distances. He raided the enemy and protected the honor of the Tonto Apache, made and repaired his own weapons and tools, and raised the heavy poles of the wickiup when the order was given to move camp. Men also dug the pit and laid the stones and fire to prepare mescal, for there was a special significance to its production that was strictly male. No one begrudged the men their few minutes in the sun each day, though the women, who had lighter tasks, found little time to sit idle.

"Tell me about that day," urged Wide Face.

"No," said Toaquin sharply. "When I returned I told the old men. Now the story is theirs to tell and they repeat it every night. Go sit at their feet if you would hear."

"But you were there. They weren't," urged Wide Face. "I'd rather hear it from you."

"I will never speak of it again." Toaquin scowled as fiercely as she could. She wished her little sister would go away and leave her to her

22

thoughts. Not that those thoughts would be pleasant. Ever since the Moon of Juniper Berries Ripening, they had been about the same thing.

"If it had been you who was stolen by the *pinda lickoyi* and not Flowering Cactus, she would tell me," said Wide Face. "She was good. You're mean, Little Gopher. You're cross and spiteful. Everybody says so. Even Flowering Cactus used to say you should be nicer to me."

It was true. How often had their elder sister chided Toaquin about her violent temper and sharp tongue. The voice of Flowering Cactus was always gentle, but the reproof was there, and each time Toaquin had promised to get better. Somehow she never did, and now it was too late. She lifted her eyes from the stone bowl to meet Wide Face's accusing stare, and it was almost as though she could hear Flowering Cactus's soft voice in her ears.

"You are the elder sister now," Flowering Cactus seemed to say. "Be kind to her, as I was kind to you. It will not harm you to tell Wide Face what happened. She has a right to hear it from you."

Toaquin looked around fearfully. The voice had been so clear. Could it have been the whisper of some spirit? Such a thing had never happened to her before, but it was safer to take no chances.

"It was in the Moon of Juniper Berries Ripening," she began grudgingly. "It was just before we came to this rancheria for the cold time. A party of gatherers were going out, and our sister, Flowering Cactus, and I went with them."

Wide Face stopped knocking her moccasined feet together and settled back to listen.

"There were nine of us, so we thought ourselves safe." Toaquin paused and regarded her sister severely. "Even with so many it is not always safe to venture far from camp. But the old one said she remembered, from her youth, a place where there were always berries, and she led us there."

Her mouth grew hard as she remembered the woman who had directed their steps to that berry patch. But for the old one's loose tongue, none of this would have happened. Flowering Cactus would still be here, smiling at Toaquin, encouraging her, offering sympathy when the others criticized, the most important person and the best beloved in Toaquin's young life. Often she had thought that Flowering Cactus was the only person in the whole band of Tonto Apaches who really loved her. And now she was gone.

"Go on," urged Wide Face, and her voice seemed to come from a great distance.

"We had to go a long way because the berries close by had been gathered," continued Toaquin slowly. "That is why we followed the old one's directions. We planned to camp all night. It was safe, we thought, with so many. Our mother told me to stay close to Flowering Cactus, and I did. Until I lost my charm."

24

"It was a special black stone, and it kept you safe from lightning." Wide Face nodded knowingly. "And it used to hang on a string about your neck, as does the one you wear now."

Toaquin frowned. If Wide Face wanted to hear the story, why didn't she keep quiet? Then she remembered that, as a good elder sister, she must cultivate patience.

"It was a powerful charm," she agreed. "It must have fallen off when we came through a thicket of brush. I remember how the bushes caught on our clothes and scratched our legs. The charm must have come off then. We came to the berry patch just beyond the brambles. As the old one said, the bushes were heavy with fruit, and at first I did not miss my charm. Then, when I did, I told Flowering Cactus. She said we would look for it later. We must pick berries first."

"But you didn't," accused Wide Face.

"Would you have?" Toaquin's temper flared instantly. "If you had lost a powerful charm that had protected you from lightning ever since you were a baby, would you have stopped to pick berries before you went to look for it?"

"No," said Wide Face meekly. "And the charm must still have been working, for if you hadn't gone back to look for it you wouldn't be here now."

Toaquin rejected the idea contemptuously. Wide Face was such a child. Black stones protected only against lightning. Everybody knew that. The fact that she was safe was just something that happened.

"I waited until Flowering Cactus and the others were picking berries," she went on, wishing their elder sister could hear how pleasantly she was talking with Wide Face. "Then I went back into the thicket. The bushes were close together, but I could see where we had broken off twigs when we came through. I was looking on the ground for my charm when I heard the noise of guns. They came from where our women were picking berries. So I crept back to look. I was careful not to make any sound, and I didn't bend the branches when I looked out. No one knew I was there."

"And you saw the *pinda lickoyi,*" promoted Wide Face, when she paused.

"There were three of them. Three white eyes," said Toaquin slowly. This was the part she didn't like to remember, the part that kept coming back to her. "They were shooting at our women, and when the children tried to run away, they shot them too. I saw one of the white eyes shoot the very old one, then he leaned down and took her hair with a sharp knife."

"Was there blood?" asked Wide Face fearfully.

"How can someone take a scalp without causing blood? The women were screaming and trying to hide the children behind them, but they couldn't get away. The white eyes just kept on shooting. I

26

saw it all." Toaquin shut her eyes. She wished she could erase the whole thing from her mind.

"I wonder what the white eyes want with hair," said Wide Face in a puzzled voice. She had heard the story so often from the old men that it had lost most of its horror for her.

"They sell it to the chief of the Mexicans," Toaquin told her. "Apache hair is called a bounty. The chief pays something called pesos for it. He pays one hundred pesos for a man's hair, and fifty pesos for a woman's, and twenty-five pesos for a child's hair."

"Is that a lot?"

"It must be or there wouldn't be so many white eyes trying to get it. They aren't all Mexicans who sell hair. The Americans sell it to the Mexican chief, too. That's one reason why we hate all white eyes."

"But they didn't cut off Flowering Cactus's hair or Gentle Rabbit's."

"No. One of the white eyes threw ropes around them so they couldn't get away. And when they left, they dragged Flowering Cactus and Gentle Rabbit along with them. Our father said they were going to make slaves of them."

Slaves! Her beloved sister a slave! The thought was more than Toaquin could bear. Great Spirit, she prayed silently, if you can't send Flowering Cactus back to me, at least send me a white eye so I may make him pay.

"Flowering Cactus had pretty hair, so long and black," said Wide Face. "And so did Gentle Rabbit. I'm glad they didn't lose it. I wonder what the chief of the Mexicans does with all that hair he buys. I wouldn't want it."

"Of course not," Toaquin told her, sniffing disdainfully. "That's why Apaches don't take hair. We have no use for it."

When she finished with the seeds, Toaquin carried them to her mother. They would be mixed with water and baked into cakes to go with the evening meal, which was now bubbling over the fire. It was squirrel meat, mixed with roots, and she sniffed enviously as she watched her mother stir the contents of the pot. Neither Toaquin nor Wide Face would be permitted any of the stew, for animal flesh was denied young girls. It had very bad effects on them and made them sick. At certain times, particularly in the event of famine, the shaman would say certain words and spells over the meat, and then it was safe for young girls to eat a little. But that did not happen very often. Toaquin would be glad when she was fully grown so she could eat meat whenever it was available.

"Sweep the ground before our wickiup," ordered She-Who-Never-Tires, her mother. "Now that you are an almost-woman, you must keep busy. It would not do for others to see you standing idle."

Toaquin fetched the length of brush that served as a broom and began dragging it across the ground. All around the circle of wickiups, girls close to her own age were doing the same thing, and soon a fine dust rose to fill the air. What grass had grown originally at the campsite was now worn away by the feet of Angry Hawk's people. The river was a sizable walk from there, so water was used sparingly, and from necessity the band was living in a world of dust.

It would be nice, Toaquin told herself, when the Smart One decided that the weather had warmed sufficiently to break this camp and move on.

"You are making a great disturbance," said a voice nearby, and Toaquin stopped stirring the dust to peer through the gritty, saffron screen.

It was Tall Piñon, a girl several years older than her. Tall Piñon had been a friend of Flowering Cactus and had recently come upon sorry times herself.

Five moons ago, Tall Piñon had been married to the young man of her choice, and they were very happy. Then one morning, he fell suddenly ill. Although the shaman did everything in his power to save him, the bridegroom was dead before the sun had closed its eye.

Tall Piñon was beside herself with grief. She cut off her hair and cried unceasingly for days, but that was not the worst. The family of her late husband did not want her, so she had to become *bijan* and return to her own parents.

There was a certain stigma about being *bijan,* which was the word used to designate young women whose husbands had divorced them or young widows. Because every *bijan* hoped to find another husband, they were usually gay and flirtatious and were receptive to male advances in a way previously unmarried girls would never be. They were not ostracized, but married women, fearing for their husbands' affections, said unkind things about them. Even girls of their own age turned against them, since a man who took a *bijan* for his wife did not have to pay so large a bride price.

It was too soon after the death of her first husband for Tall Piñon to desire another, but Toaquin knew her family was already urging it upon her. She thought that would be very unpleasant.

"I can't sweep without making dust," she reminded the older girl. "I hope our Smart One will move the camp soon. No matter how hard we try to keep it clean, we can't do it. It smells."

"The sun gathers warmth each day," said Tall Piñon. "And the next camping place will doubtless be by the river. You'll like that, won't you?"

"In a way," agreed Toaquin. Living by the river had its disadvantages, too. Every morning at dawn, Apache children were required to run to the stream and jump into the icy water. It was said to give them strength.

"A runner is coming! A runner is coming!" The shout came from beyond the circle of wickiups, behind the place where the men were now sitting in the shade. "He is one of ours."

"Perhaps it's news from Bad Heart," cried Toaquin hopefully. She thrust the end of the brush broom into the ground and used it to help her jump up and down, the way younger children used their shinny sticks.

"Do you think so?" There was such a note of alarm in Tall Piñon's voice that Toaquin stopped hopping and looked at her in surprise.

"It's time. They have been gone two moons, nearly three."

"But perhaps they weren't successful," said Tall Piñon. "Raiding parties aren't always successful."

"The runner will tell us when he gets here." Toaquin continued to stare at the older girl in amazement. Could it be possible that Tall Piñon hoped the returning braves had been defeated?

"I must go now," said Tall Piñon nervously. "I must take this water to my mother."

Toaquin watched the slim figure in the new buckskin skirt and tunic, which had been hastily made after the recent funeral, disappear into the camp dust. What could be the matter with Tall Piñon? For weeks after her young husband had

31

gone to the Ghost Chief, she had been disconsolate. She had cut her hair and slashed her clothes and poured ashes over herself time and again, although one pouring of ashes on the day the body was laid to rest was quite enough. After that she grew calmer, and today, when she stopped to chat with Toaquin, Tall Piñon had seemed almost like her old self. It was not until the crier announced the coming of a runner that she changed.

Toaquin put the matter from her mind. She had more important things to think about. She gave a last flick at the ground with her brush broom, then hurried to join the crowd that was gathering to await the arrival of the runner.

Before long they could see him, loping easily along at the edge of the desert, a dot that grew larger and larger until it assumed the shape of a man.

"It's Throws-a-Rope." Someone recognized him, and soon everyone could see for himself.

Throws-a-Rope was one of the youngest of the Tonto Apaches who had acccompanied Bad Heart on the raid. As yet, he was not a recognized warrior, but he had asked to go and had been accepted. In a tribe known for its fleet runners, Throws-a-Rope was the fastest, and now those months and years of practicing when he was a boy were paying off. To Throws-a-Rope belonged the honor of bringing news of the raiding mission.

When he arrived, the young man appeared

32

hardly winded, although Toaquin knew he was. It was self-control and training that kept Throws-a-Rope's voice steady.

"Our mission was successful," he told Angry Hawk, the Tonto chief, who stepped forward to receive him. "We overtook a party of white eyes, and now Bad Heart and the others who suffered losses the day our women gathered berries are avenged. They are one sleep behind me and will tell you so themselves at the next sun."

Angry Hawk nodded, and the Tonto Apaches murmured their approval.

"It was not a rich raid. Only one wagon," reported Throws-a-Rope regretfully. "But the warriors bring some prizes. Blankets and kettles, knives and a gun and bullets. And the meat from the animals that pulled the white eyes' wagon."

"It is welcome news," said Angry Hawk. Then raising his voice, he called out, "Let all the *bijans* prepare themselves. Since they have no men to provide for them, they will want to dance for the returning warriors and be rewarded with gifts."

At that, Toaquin knew the reason for Tall Piñon's behavior. This was the first raiding party to return since she had lost her husband and was eligible to marry again. It would be her first dance, and dance she must. But at least, Toaquin thought, she need not dance alone. There were half a dozen *bijans* in the camp. On such occasions, the *bijans* painted their bodies white and wore only strips of cloth across their breasts and hips. Toaquin felt a little sorry for Tall Piñon. The Apaches were modest people. Their bodies were always covered. To dance this way would be difficult for anyone, especially the first time. Then she reminded herself that it was better than being a slave like Flowering Cactus. At least Tall Piñon was among her own people.

"Like the party of white eyes who killed our women, Bad Heart has taken two captives, two girl children," concluded Throws-a-Rope. "He says that he will give one to our leader, the Smart One, and the other to Shakes-His-Lance, to repay for the loss of his daughter, Flowering Cactus."

A slave, thought Toaquin wildly. The Great Spirit had heard her prayer. Her father, Shakes-His-Lance, was being given a slave to make up for Flowering Cactus. As if anything could make up for the loss of her beloved sister, she told herself angrily. But at least it was in her power to make this white eye suffer, just as Flowering Cactus might be suffering this very minute.

Chapter 3

"Y OKIA," ORDERED THE INDIAN, ROUGHLY kicking Olive with his moccasin toe.

Although her bones ached and her feet burned and stung painfully, she managed to stand up. She knew nothing of the Apache language, but she had decided that the word *yokia,* used so often in the past days meant "go on" or "hurry up."

Mary Ann, who had been lying on the ground beside her, refused to respond to repeated kicks, and after a minute or two the Apache grunted in disgust before he picked her up and slung her over his shoulder. He had been carrying her for days.

Olive looked at her little sister's head, bobbing against the leather shirt, and she made herself squeeze back tears. She wouldn't let these dirty savages see her cry again. Poor Mary Ann, so little and frail! Olive would have to be both mother and father to her now. And she would! Everything that Ma had taught her, everything that she had learned in her own twelve years she'd pass along to Mary Ann.

She took her assigned place in the line of Apaches, and when they moved forward, she walked too, trying to ignore the burning soreness of her feet. She must not think of them. She must think of other things instead.

As usual, her thoughts returned to that awful night when the Indians had attacked the wagon. The Apaches had stripped it of all its valuables. Almost everything had been taken: what little food remained and the pots to cook it in, tools and Pa's gun, clothing, especially shoes, which the Indians ripped from the feet of their victims, blankets and quilts, bits of iron and metal, even the canvas top of the wagon itself. They had slashed Ma's featherbed to see what it contained, and the goose down and feathers had risen in the air, settling softly on all those motionless figures on the ground.

Olive had cried bitterly as she watched. That wanton destruction had been especially hard to bear. Ma had worked for years collecting all the down and feathers to fill the mattress, and in a few minutes it was gone, gathered by the wind and carried in every direction.

But Ma would not need it now. She was dead. They were all dead, everyone but Mary Ann and herself. They would never build New Zion as Pa had planned or feel the warmth of the sun or the coolness of a wind again. Of course, they were with God. Olive did not doubt that for a moment. And perhaps that was better than building a New Zion on the banks of an earthly river. God must have thought so, or He wouldn't have permitted this terrible thing to happen. Obviously, He wasn't ready for Olive or Mary Ann, or He would have taken them too.

As she plodded along behind the brown Apache back, occasionally spurred on by a kick from the Indian who followed, Olive wondered how much farther they must travel. That first night, when she and Mary Ann had sobbed over the loss of their family, the Apaches had thought it was funny. Then they had grown irritated with these displays of grief. At the sight of flourished war clubs, Olive managed to stifle her cries, although Mary Ann continued to weep silently.

They had traveled all night, and by the next morning they were so exhausted there was no time to think of anything but their own physical discomfort. The Apaches had taken their shoes, and the rough stones of the mountains they climbed in darkness soon lacerated their tender, bare feet. Olive had been given pieces of leather to tie onto her soles, but by that time Mary Ann had collapsed from weakness and was being carried. Rest periods were brief—no more than an hour—and far between, but the hardest thing to endure was hunger, for they ate but once a day.

Before they left, the Indians had slaughtered the cattle. Each man carried some of the meat, and strips of that, broiled over a fire, with hard cakes made from the last of the Oatmans' flour mixed with water and baked in the ashes, constituted the daily meal.

The first time they ate, Olive observed that there was some dispute about what should be served to the captives. Some of the party seemed to feel that the girls should have only flour cakes, while others argued that they be given strips of meat as well. Finally the man whom she took to be the leader settled the matter by handing each girl a small piece of meat. It was half raw and unsalted. Moreover, it was from one of their own friendly oxen that had pulled them so patiently all the way from Illinois, but at the time neither stopped to think of that. They gobbled it down as quickly as they could and nearly broke their teeth on the hard flour cake, hoping there would be a second helping, but there wasn't. The Apaches were tireless on the trail and ate sparingly.

Twice they were joined briefly by small bands of Indians who seemed to be known to their captors. One of these drew his bow, and the arrow pierced the long folds of Olive's skirt. He was not allowed to take second aim. The leader of the Tonto Apaches put his own body in front of the girls, while others disarmed the attacker. There were angry shouts and what sounded like abusive language, and before long the strangers left camp.

Olive had been very frightened when it happened, but as she remembered it now, it was just part of one continuous nightmare. She had lost track of time and had no idea how many days they had been traveling.

Most of their journey had been through mountainous terrain, but now she was aware that the ground beneath her aching feet was level. She looked up and saw that they were on the edge of a desert. Far ahead was a line of rocky cliffs, and to her right lay stretches of sand with only occasional clumps of sage and cactus.

Although no one spoke, she could sense a new spirit among her captors. Their shoulders straightened beneath the heavy packs. The black eyes in the dirty brown faces seemed to brighten. The moccasined feet moved forward with new briskness, so that it was hard for her to keep up.

"I think we're almost there, wherever we're going," she called to Mary Ann.

Mary Ann lifted her head and looked at Olive through glazed eyes in a dirty face. Olive made herself smile reassuringly. Oh, if only Ma were here to tell her what to do! Mary Ann looked sick, like she had a fever coming on. She ought to be put to bed under some warm quilts with some nice, nourishing beef tea to drink.

"*Yokia,*" said the man behind, adding a fresh bruise to her leg with the hard toe of his moccasin.

The clear air made distances deceptive. It was almost noon before they reached the line of brown cliffs that had looked so close. By that time Olive was panting with heat and exertion. She didn't know how she could keep going much longer. Several times she had considered falling down and saying she could go no farther, but she didn't. She knew what would happen. They would beat her until she did go on.

It was almost a surprise when she found they had arrived at their destination. She had been looking at her feet, willing herself not to stumble, and when she glanced up, the brown cliffs were rearing above their heads. At their base was a cluster of low huts, each with an opening near the ground.

Their approach to the village had been made in silence, and until their arrival, it was greeted in the same way. Then, without warning, there was noise, so much noise that it made her ears ring. Voices shouted and there was the frenzied beating of drums. She felt herself being lifted in the air, and then sticks were poking into her sides. She had been thrown onto a heap of brush, and the next moment Mary Ann came tumbling down beside her.

"Where are we?" demanded Mary Ann fearfully.

"I don't know. I think it's where they live." Olive wrinkled her nose in distaste at the smell that hung over the encampment. It was composed of dust and refuse, a place where many people had lived too long.

"Why did they put us up here?" asked Mary Ann. "These sticks are poking into me."

"I don't know," admitted Olive. She tried to break off some of the protruding branches to make their seat a little more comfortable, but it was no use. "Maybe it's because they want us where everybody can see us," she suggested. "After all, we're new. Maybe they've never seen white people before."

She was glad that Mary Ann accepted the explanation, but she didn't believe it herself. She had suddenly remembered reading about Indians burning captives at the stake. Of course, a brush pile wasn't a stake, but it would serve the same purpose. She put her arms around her little sister and held her as close as possible.

"I'm hungry," said Mary Ann fretfully. "When will they have supper?"

"Probably soon," Olive told her soothingly. "They want to greet their friends first, and then, of course, they have to cook it. Why don't you close your eyes and get a little rest?"

Mary Ann nodded and closed her eyes obediently, while Olive looked fearfully on the ground below. If they were to be burned, it would come later. The raiding party was busy talking to those who had stayed at home, obviously boasting of the recent success. The spoils taken from the Oatman wagon were placed in a pile, but from time to time the returning raiders pointed toward the girls atop the heap of brush. Their gestures were clear. The captives were the greatest prize.

"Look down there," whispered Mary Ann, and Olive realized it was too much to expect her to sleep at a time like this. "Those children. They're not any older than us. Maybe they'll help us."

A group of children had left the larger crowd of adults and now clustered at the base of the brush pile. There were girls as well as boys, and Olive didn't think any could be older than eight or ten. But as she stared at the brown faces glaring upward, she knew there was no help to be found there. These were angry faces, each one filled with hatred. Even the youngest, the two- and three-year-olds, were unsmiling.

The next moment something warm and damp

struck her arm, and then the air was filled with moisture. With the aid of curved sticks that enabled them to jump higher into the air, the Apache children were spitting at them.

"Stop it," cried Mary Ann indignantly. "That's not nice."

"Cover your face," said Olive, dropping her head into her calico lap. "They'll run out of spit after a while."

When they grew tired of spitting, the children threw dirt. They kept that up until the pounding of drums began again. The dirt-throwing stopped abruptly. Olive waited a few moments before lifting her head to see what had called their tormentors away.

Three men were pounding on large stones with some sort of clubs. Others were drawing short strings across pieces of distended bark. These gave off shrill, piping notes and made her think of the fiddlers at home. Of course, an expert fiddler could draw real tunes from his violin, while all these savages were able to achieve was a series of discordant sounds.

The Apaches began forming a circle around the brush heap, and before long they were performing what Olive supposed they called dancing. There seemed to be no accepted step. Some gyrated rapidly, executing many small circles within the larger one, while others shuffled more slowly. And while they danced, they kept up what she considered a terrible caterwauling of shrieks and yells. Men, women, and children, regardless of age, joined in the performance, and as they passed the place on the brush pile where Mary Ann and Olive sat, everyone looked up and gave an especially loud scream. There was no sign of friendliness anywhere, and those who smiled did so in a way that made the girls cling closely together.

"Look," whispered Mary Ann in awe. "Some of them don't have any clothes on."

Olive took one glance, then tried to avert her eyes. Several of the women were dancing almost naked. They had painted their bodies white and wore only wisps of cloth across their breasts and small wisps about their hips.

"Don't look at them," she advised her sister quickly. "They're not decent."

But it was hard not to look, for the white-painted women were the gayest, most abandoned of the dancers. From time to time one of them would leave the ring to dart over to the newly returned raiders, who were observing as spectators. Sometimes she would be given something from the pile of goods belonging to the Oatmans. Then, with loud shrieks of delight, she would return to the circle and continue her dancing.

"When will it be over?" asked Mary Ann finally.

Olive shook her head. She figured it had been noon when they arrived, and although the sun had now dropped below the face of the cliff, leaving everything in shadows, the dancers showed no signs of tiring. But at least, she told herself, they hadn't set fire to the pile of brush. Not yet, anyway.

The festivities continued until well after dark. Most of the loot from the wagon had been given away by that time. Many of the white-painted ladies had disappeared, much to Olive's relief, in the company of the returning raiders. Only one or two of the warriors continued to watch the dancing.

One of these was the leader who had given them strips of meat on the journey. When he suddenly held up his hand, the drummers stopped beating on their rocks, and the musicians ceased drawing strings across the pieces of bark.

Everything was quiet as he stalked over to the pile of brush. With one arm, he jerked Mary Ann from her uncertain perch and began dragging her across the dusty ground toward a tall Indian who had stepped out of the circle.

Olive cried out and would have followed her sister, but two Apaches jumped forward and held her fast. Above the pounding of her own heart, she could hear the voice of the leader of the raiding party. He spoke loudly and went on and on, as though he might be making a speech. The people listened eagerly. From time to time, some of them would nod, as though expressing approval.

When he finished, the speaker thrust Mary Ann

forward, and she fell on the ground at the feet of the tall Apache. A woman dressed in fringed deerskin stepped forward and pulled the little girl to her feet. A moment later the two had been swallowed up by the crowd.

"Mary Ann!" cried Olive wildly. "Mary Ann, where are you?"

There was no answer, nor was she given time to think of her sister further. The leader of the raiding party had returned for her. She, too, was dragged across the circle, and this time a different man stepped forward to receive her. He was not so tall as the first, and his stern face was crossed with many lines. He had black, frightening eyes, and his thin mouth was a straight, unrelenting line.

Again the leader made a speech, and all the time the man to whom it was directed kept those frightening black eyes on Olive's face. He hates me, she thought, and I never did anything to him. Why should he hate me so?

When he had finished speaking, the leader of the raiding party pushed Olive forward roughly. She stumbled, but unlike Mary Ann she did not fall. For just a second she was quite close to the Apache, and he stepped back, frowning, as though she might be something that was unclean to the touch.

He barked out a word that she could not understand, and in answer a girl stepped out of the ranks of women behind. She was younger than Olive by at least a year, and much slighter. She wore the traditional fringed garments of Apache women, and on a string about her neck dangled a black stone.

When she saw her, Olive's spirits lifted a little. Perhaps she was going to be placed in the custody of someone who would prove a friend. The feeling left as she saw the expression in the girl's eyes. They were as filled with anger and loathing as those of the man.

"Toaquin," said the girl, pointing to herself. Then, grasping the white girl's arm with fingers that were surprisingly strong and unyielding, she uttered the one word in Apache that Olive had learned. *"Yokia."*

Chapter 4

THE MOMENT SHE AWOKE, TOAQUIN THOUGHT of the two white eye slaves. That was not unusual since she thought of them most of the time. What could she do today to make their lives uncomfortable? If only she knew what their captors were doing to Flowering Cactus and Gentle Rabbit, it would make things easier. Then she could do the same things to Mary and Olive.

Mary and Olive. Olive and Mary. She repeated the words silently in an effort to wear them out. But it wasn't the same as though she could say them aloud. To do that now might awaken the others sleeping in the wickiup.

She used the white eyes' names as often as possible. Any name that was overused lost its power. A warrior, who had been careful with his name, could shout it in battle, and the word would bring him hidden strength. The ignorant white eyes did not know that. When Toaquin called them by name, they smiled timidly, probably thinking she was being kind.

Today, she decided, Olive and Mary would spend the early hours digging roots. Roots were growing hard to find. Perhaps she would give them two of the babies to tend at the same time. It was harder to stoop and dig with a wicker cradle strapped to one's back. Later, when the sun was hot, they would pick mesquite. The berries were just beginning to ripen, and it would be tedious work, selecting ripe berries from the green. And they would have a scanty breakfast, too. Toaquin would see to that. The slaves ate after the Apaches had finished. Even in the unlikely event that she must gorge herself, Toaquin would make sure that not much was left over. She doubted if Flowering Cactus and Gentle Rabbit were given much to eat.

She now had Mary in her charge as well as Olive, two slaves on whom to vent her anger.

Five moons ago, when Bad Heart brought the girls to camp, the one called Mary was found to be filled with devils of sickness. Running Deer, wife of Angry Hawk, to whom she had been given, did not force her to go with the others to dig roots or to carry wood or water. Of course, no shaman was summoned to drive the devils out, but when the band moved out of winter quarters, the slave rode on a drag. Toaquin, walking with the women, writhed in anger.

Although he was paid nothing, the shaman gave his opinion. Mary's time was short. Soon she would be summoned by the Ghost Chief, and it was not worth their while to take her with them. Running Deer took her anyway.

"Perhaps this girl child will win her own battle with the devils," she insisted. "Then she will be of much use to me. Besides, she is brave. She has not complained, although the devils must be causing great pain. They shake her by the shoulders every time she coughs."

"That is true," agreed the older Apache woman. Bravery was something to be admired. "We have not heard her cry out or whimper once."

At the time, Toaquin had not thought much about it. She was too busy with her father's slave, who had been placed in her charge. It was she who assigned the daily tasks that began at sunup and lasted well into the night. At first the white eye was stupid about them. She did not even know the proper roots or how to dig them. She did not know the right kind of wood to gather, and it was impossible for her to carry a heavy jar of water with-

50

out spilling it. She did not even know how to take a baby from his woven cradle or change the soft, shredded bark lining in which he was wrapped beneath the top covering of rabbit skin. She knew nothing. Toaquin had to teach her. The instruction was enjoyable because Toaquin could accompany it with stinging slaps and loud-voiced comments that brought the other children to stand and jeer.

With every blow and each abusive word, Toaquin thought of her own sister, who was also a slave. That's for you, Flowering Cactus, she told herself silently. Maybe you'll never know, but I'm paying back some of what they're doing to you.

After they reached their first summer camping place, the slave named Mary seemed to rally. The devils of sickness had decided she was not worth their while, and they went away. She had been given a little meat broth, and once Running Deer insisted that she have stew made from rabbit and acorn meal. She was very thin and teetered as she walked, and her cough remained, but she was able to do a little work.

Soon, Running Deer promised, she would let Toaquin take Mary as well as Olive when they gathered roots and berries. Toaquin could hardly wait.

But when the day came, it was a disappointment. In some way, Olive must have instructed her sister in the manner of digging roots and the proper ones to choose. Although Mary panted and coughed a great deal, she hurried from task to task, gathering wood, carrying water, changing babies in their cradles without a word of protest and in a way that warranted few reprimands. Worst of all, the children who had once come running to watch while Toaquin screamed abuse and rained blows on the elder slave had lost interest. Now they didn't even look up from their play.

Suddenly Toaquin was aware that light was filtering through the brush laid against the poles of the summer wickiup. The sun would be up any moment. She scrambled to her feet and touched her sleeping sister, Wide Face, on the shoulder. Wide Face stirred and mumbled under her breath, but she did not argue. As the two girls crept toward the door opening, Toaquin squinted across the shadowy interior. The places opposite, where her brothers slept, were already deserted. It must be later than she had thought.

Olive was not permitted to sleep inside the family wickiup. She was expected to make her bed on the ground outside the entrance. As she passed, Toaquin kicked at her.

"Get up, lazy slave. Get up, Olive," she ordered. "Take your root basket and see what you and Mary can find."

"It's still—" The protest was begun before Olive was quite awake. The next moment she began scrambling to her feet.

"Olive," said Toaquin carefully. Then she added for good measure, "Olive, Olive, Olive!" That's for you, Flowering Cactus, she told herself. Soon there will be no power in the name at all.

"I wish we didn't have to do this every day," complained Wide Face, as they trotted down the path that Tonto Apache moccasins had worn to the river. "It's always so cold in the morning."

"That's why we do it," Toaquin explained irritably. Surely her sister was old enough to understand that. But for the sake of Flowering Cactus, she tried to be patient. "The cold water gives strength to our bodies. If we jumped in the river when the day is hot, what good would it do to us?"

"It would make us cool," said Wide Face. "Let's not stay in very long."

"We'll stay as long as the others," insisted Toaquin firmly. She, too, hoped it would not be long, but she consoled herself with the knowledge that the slaves would like nothing better than to dip themselves in the river. Olive had once asked permission to take a bath. Toaquin, who had been about to order her to do just that, turned down the request immediately. Flowering Cactus was undoubtedly denied the privilege of bathing in a river.

Olive and Mary returned at midmorning with only a few roots in their baskets. Toaquin, who suspected they had eaten most of what they had dug, recommended a beating, but Running Deer intervened.

"It is late for roots," she insisted. "Even the leaves are dry and have returned to the earth mother. The slaves did well to find these."

She-Who-Never-Tires, too, sided against her daughter.

"It would have been better to set them the tasks of carrying wood and water," she told Toaquin reprovingly. "Wood and water are always needed. And if the hunters return successful, we shall need even more."

Toaquin drooped her head resentfully. Why were people always criticizing her? Why could she never do anything to please? Sometimes it seemed to her that everyone was against her. In Angry Hawk's whole band, she couldn't name a single friend. If only Flowering Cactus were here, she would understand.

The morning meal was boiled meat and ground meal for the adults and meal cakes for young girls. Today there was also a delicacy, roasted grasshoppers, in which everyone could join, since grasshoppers were not flesh. There was one meal cake apiece for the slaves, and there would have been a few grasshoppers left over, but Toaquin made sure that some of the Apache children ate them.

After it was finished, she led her two charges to where the mesquite bushes were growing close to camp.

"Do you like living here with us, Olive?" she asked, once she had ordered the girls to gather only ripe berries and leave the green ones for a later picking.

For a moment Olive pretended not to understand, although Toaquin was sure she did. Both girls had picked up the Apache tongue in an amazingly short time, although there were some words that seemed difficult for them to pronounce.

"Are you happy living with us?" repeated Toaquin, frowning.

"We miss our parents, our father and mother, and our sisters and brothers," answered Olive after a moment.

"I, too, miss my sister. She is a slave, a slave of the white eyes, just as you are a slave of ours," said Toaquin. Then she added hastily, "Olive."

"I'm sorry about your sister. But she must be a slave of the Mexicans, not the Americans."

"Don't Americans have slaves, Olive?"

"The only slaves are black people. Negroes. And that's only in one part of the country. Americans don't have slaves where we live."

"How many Americans are there, Olive?"

"Thousands and thousands. More than the berries on this bush."

"You are a liar, Olive," Toaquin told her angrily. "All Americans are liars. There are only a few of them. But those few have guns and horses. How did they get guns and horses, Olive? Where did they find those riches? And why do they come to the land of the Apache? Why are they so wicked?"

"They aren't all wicked," protested Mary, joining in the conversation.

"They are all wicked. An evil spirit leads them. Once they invited one of our chiefs—I cannot say his name because he has gone to join the Ghost Chief—and his braves to a feast. And the meat the white eyes gave our people to eat that day was poison. Not one Apache walked away."

"That was wicked," agreed Mary Ann, her eyes filling with tears. "It is better to be friends."

"Friends? When Mangas Coloradas, the great chief of the Warm Spring Apaches, went to offer help and friendship to the Americans, do you know what happened, Mary? Do you know, Olive?"

The girls shook their heads.

"One of the white eyes struck him again and again with a long whip, Olive. That is the way Americans treat an offer of friendship."

Olive did not answer. She continued picking berries steadily. Mary Ann, however, paused to wipe her eyes. Since Running Deer was not there to prevent it, Toaquin gave her a quick slap on the side of her head. Somehow it made her feel better.

When they returned to camp with their baskets of mesquite berries, it was to find visitors. A handful of Mohaves were sitting, smoking and drinking *tulibai* with Angry Hawk and some of his elders. The women were scurrying around, preparing a proper meal for guests, and the children had stopped their play to stand as close as they dared and observe the strangers.

It was not often that Angry Hawk's band had visitors. As a group they were a quarrelsome lot and had broken off from the larger band of Tonto Apaches so that they might be by themselves and make their own rules. They had little in common with the other Apache—the Chiricahua, the Mimbreno, the Bedonkohe, or other Warm Springs tribes. Nowadays the only Indians with whom they maintained commerce were the unrelated Mohaves, who lived on the sandy bottoms of the Colorado River three hundred miles away.

Toaquin sent the slaves to attend the row of babies swinging in their cradles from the branches of trees, while she herself offered her services to her mother. She-Who-Never-Tires was busy at the cooking fire. It was not far from the circle of men, and Toaquin was eager for any scrap of news the strangers might have brought with them.

Naturally, She-Who-Never-Tires would not let her young daughter help with the stew. Toaquin was not only too young to eat flesh, she was too young to prepare it. But there were other tasks that needed doing. First, there was the need for more water.

"Go to the river," ordered She-Who-Never-Tires. "Quickly. Had you sent the slaves this morning, you would not have to go yourself."

For a moment Toaquin considered calling Olive or Mary away from the babies. Then she decided against it. It was not far to the river. She could be there and back by the time she freed one of the slaves from baby tending.

As she started out with her pottery jar, she encountered Tall Piñon, bent on the same errand. In the months since they had left winter quarters, Tall Piñon had changed. She no longer wept, and her black hair had grown to cover her ears. Of course, she would always be too tall for beauty and her bones were very close to the skin, but looking at her now, Toaquin thought that Tall Piñon was almost pretty.

"You look happy," she said, falling in behind the older girl on the path. "Can I guess why?"

"By now everyone can guess," admitted Tall Piñon. "I thought it would never happen to me. I thought no one would ever want me but my husband who went to join the Ghost Chief."

"Bad Heart does," said Toaquin. She thought back to the night when Tall Piñon had made her first dance, painted white, as a *bijan*. "You had hardly danced the circle when he came and threw a blanket about your shoulders."

"That was to cover my shame." Tall Piñon

$miled. "He is a kind man, a brave warrior. But he is also shy. It was only in this moon that he found courage to come to my father's wickiup, and we sat facing each other. Tonight he will offer *itsa*, the dowry, and I am sure my father will accept."

"You must be very happy," said Toaquin. She wondered if somewhere in a distant land some man would ever offer a dowry for the slave, Flowering Cactus.

It was not until late at night that Toaquin received an inkling of the discussion held between the visitors and the elders of the tribe. Of course, there had been plenty of opportunity to inspect the pile of produce they had brought to trade—squash and corn, melons and grain. They had been placed in a great heap beside Angry Hawk's wickiup, and it made her mouth water in anticipation. Sometimes Toaquin wished that her own people grew these wondrous things. But Apaches were not farmers. They were hunters and warriors. Tomorrow there would be an exchange of furs and hides and arrowheads for the produce of the fields, and that was as it should be.

When Shakes-His-Lance finally returned to the wickiup, a little tipsy from the *tulibai* he had drunk, he was unusually talkative.

"The Mohaves say their chief might be interested in trading for the two white eye slaves," he announced. "He might even give as much as a horse, and he would certainly give a few blankets."

"A horse is a good thing," replied She-Who-Never-Tires practically. "And we always need blankets."

Anger rose within Toaquin, and her heart began to beat wildly. Why, she had hardly begun to avenge her sister, Flowering Cactus. The slaves musn't be traded away!

Chapter 5

O H, I'M SO HUNGRY," SAID MARY ANN. "IF I could just have a big cup of bread and milk!"

"Here," said her sister quickly. "This is the biggest root I've found this morning. See how fat it is? Eat it, Mary Ann. It will make you feel better."

"Nothing will make me feel better until I get something good to eat." Mary Ann popped the fat root into her mouth and chewed busily. "I'll have another," she decided.

"We musn't eat too many," cautioned Olive. "I think Toaquin's guessed that we've been eating roots when we go out to dig."

"That Toaquin," said Mary Ann bitterly. "I've tried to be nice to her, but she won't let me. I think she hates us more than anybody. Why didn't she come with us this morning?"

"Her mother is helping her make a new dress. It's for some kind of heathen ceremony. Toaquin says that soon she will be a woman and that for several days she'll be the most important person in the camp."

"Maybe that would be a good time for us to escape," said Mary Ann slowly. "Everybody would be busy."

The same thought had occurred to Olive. With Toaquin too busy to think of them, it would have been an ideal opportunity for escape. They might even get a day's head start before the Apaches discovered they were missing. If Olive had been alone, she would have taken the chance. Every night she dreamed of getting away, of returning to a white society. The slights and slurs she had experienced in Illinois were nothing compared to this. But she wasn't alone. She must think of Mary Ann first, and her little sister wouldn't be able to travel fast or far.

"As soon as you're strong enough, we'll try," she promised. "But you've been sick. We'd probably have to walk a long way."

"I walked back to this camp," said Mary Ann defensively. "I'm getting stronger every day."

Olive failed to point out that on their return to the Apache's winter quarters, Running Deer had made sure Mary Ann's walk was broken several times a day by a ride on one of the travois pulled by horses. In the nine months they had been captives, the chief's wife had intervened several times on Mary Ann's behalf. Toaquin was not allowed to beat her as she did Olive, and on cold nights Mary Ann slept inside the chief's wickiup, not outside the closed flap, which was the accustomed sleeping place for slaves. Olive was grateful to Running Deer. Without her help, she would never have been able to protect her little sister as she should.

"I'm perfectly well now," continued Mary Ann stubbornly. "We can run away any time."

"We have to make plans first," Olive told her cautiously. She didn't want to discourage her. Ma had always said man lived on hope, and she wouldn't want to take that away from Mary Ann. "We don't even know which way to start out. I listen all the time; you must too. If we hear of a wagon train, we've got to find out where it is and how long it would take us to get there."

"Oh, I can do that," cried Mary Ann eagerly. "I've learned to talk Apache real good, and Running Deer tells me lots of things. Pretty soon I'll be as smart as a real Apache."

Oh, dear God, don't let her turn into an Indian, thought Olive. Mary Ann's so young. It would be easy for her to forget everything she used to know.

"If we want to get back to our own people," she continued, trying to keep her voice steady, "we've got to be very careful. We can't make any mistakes. It's like a game."

Mary Ann nodded and her eyes sparkled. She loved games.

"We'd have to have a little food to take," continued Olive. "We wouldn't have time to stop and find it on the way. And we'd have to cover our trail. You know what good trackers the Indians are. And the wagon train would have to be pretty close. I couldn't carry you, the way the Apaches did when they brought us here."

"You wouldn't have to. This time it would be different," argued Mary Ann. "We wouldn't be barefoot. We have moccasins now. And we don't wear long dresses to catch on things."

Olive forced herself to smile, but she didn't feel like it. The Apaches had taken their clothing, replacing it with skin skirts and tunics. Once they must have belonged to someone else, for they were old and the leather was wearing thin in spots. Mary Ann hadn't minded the exchange. She thought it was fun to dress up like an Indian. But Olive had given up her long dress and petticoats reluctantly. They were a link to civilization, to the life she had known and to which she so desperately wanted to return.

But she had told the truth when she said they must make preparations. Escape was not so easy as Mary Ann believed. They didn't know which way to go to find people of their own race. If they started out blindly, the Apaches would find them and bring them back. Worst of all was Mary Ann's health. Despite her protests, she wasn't strong, and she still had that cough. Besides, she was barely eight. Without a calendar, they couldn't celebrate her birthday, but it had been in the summer. All sorts of things could happen. One of them could fall and break a bone, or they could be attacked by wild animals, or starve to death. Olive was careful not to say any of these things aloud, but she knew that they dare not make the attempt now.

"Maybe those Mohaves who visited the summer camp a while ago will buy us," suggested Mary Ann brightly. "Running Deer says if they offer enough, Angry Hawk will sell us."

"Do you think that would be any better?" Olive worked rapidly with her digging stick, jabbing it into the ground and using it as a lever to bring up the root. They were lucky today. They had found a thick patch, and their baskets were nearly full. They would have been completely full by this time if they hadn't eaten so many. But the roots might be their only breakfast, since girls were denied meat. Often there was nothing left over after the Apaches had finished their own meal.

"The Mohaves can't be any worse," declared Mary Ann. "They probably live better than the Apaches. At least they grow vegetables. That's what they brought to trade. The only thing is"— she paused to look longingly at an exceptionally round root before dropping it into her basket— "they live so far away. Maybe as much as three hundred miles. I don't think I could walk that far."

"Then how do you think we could escape?" asked Olive practically. "We might have to walk farther than that to find our own people."

Mary Ann was prevented from replying by a fit of coughing. Olive watched her anxiously. Ma had always said Mary Ann would die of consumption. Olive wasn't quite sure what consumption was, but she was certain it was worse than a cough.

She listened to the racking cough go on and on, wondering what Ma would do for it. A mustard plaster, maybe, or a tonic. But Olive had neither of those. All she could do was wait for the cough to wear itself out. As she looked at her sister, she thought how pretty Mary Ann was getting. Her eyes looked very bright and shiny and her skin was translucent. She was very thin, but that was because she was always hungry. Olive was hungry too.

"My basket's full," she said after a while. "I'll

help you fill yours, then we'd better go back. I don't want Toaquin to come looking for us."

When the girls arrived in camp, they could see that something out of the ordinary had occurred. Apaches were running here and there, shouting and laughing. The cooking fires had been built up, although it was early for the morning meal.

"It must be company," said Mary Ann, and Olive nodded. She had already noticed extra horses hobbled with the band that belonged to the Tonto Apaches.

Running Deer came hurrying up to them.

"Come into my wickiup," she ordered, taking Mary Ann's basket of roots and motioning for Wide Face, who was standing nearby, to take Olive's. "You are needed. I was about to send for you."

"What is it?" asked Olive. "What has happened?"

"You are being traded," taunted Wide Face. "Toaquin is angry, but I'm glad. I'm glad not to have to look at the ugly white eyes anymore."

Running Deer shoved her away with enough force to make Wide Face stumble, but not enough to upset the basket. She scampered off, shrieking, "I'm glad!" and the other children nearby took up the chant.

"Inside," said Running Deer again, pushing them toward the door opening.

It was dusky within, and for a moment Olive

67

thought they were alone. Then she saw there was a girl sitting on the dirt floor, a girl a few years older than herself. She had long black hair and wore no upper garment, only a skirt of shredded bark, which extended from her waist to her knees. Her skin was clear and brown, and her face would have been pretty if it had not been for lines of blue tattooing on her chin. Around her neck were strands of white and blue beads, and apparently she had been given food upon her arrival for she was rapidly devouring the contents of a pottery bowl.

"These are the slaves," announced Running Deer proudly. "The younger one is mine. She has a good disposition and does not cry or whine. I am sorry that my husband wants to trade her. She is called Mary. The elder is called Olive. She belongs to our *nantas,* the second in command, Shakes-His-Lance."

The visitor scraped the sides of her bowl and licked her fingers. She examined each girl in turn. Olive was surprised to see her smile. It had been a long time since anyone had smiled at her.

"I am Topeka," she announced in the Apache tongue. "My father is Espaniol, chief of the Mohaves."

"You will find them good workers," continued Running Deer. "Mary is not so quick as Olive, but that is because she is young. As she grows, she may be even quicker."

"They are very thin," observed Topeka. "I see their bones."

"All white eyes are thin," Running Deer insisted. "It is the way they are. Have you ever seen a fat white eye?"

"No," said Topeka. "But I have only seen two, and never a white eye woman."

"The women are all thin," said Running Deer positively. "Much thinner than the men. But strong."

Olive knew that Running Deer had never seen a white woman except for herself and Mary Ann, but she did not say so. The Mohave girl looked kind. At least she had smiled at them.

"You will take them?" asked Running Deer. "Having two white eye slaves will bring much honor to your father. Everyone will know he is a great man when they see these slaves working for him."

"I will take them," agreed Topeka. "Tonight we will rest with our friends, the Apaches, but at sunup we will leave for the country of the Mohaves. The slaves will go with us."

That evening, while the men were drinking *tulibai* in honor of their guests, Toaquin came to the shadowy place, away from the fire, where Olive and Mary Ann were sitting. For once their hands were idle, for Toaquin had been too busy to assign tasks. No one else had time to think of them. The elder women were entertaining Topeka, daughter of the Mohave chief, asking questions, gathering what news they could of a world beyond their tiny sphere. The children were busy, too. They dared not crowd too close to either circle, but they went from one to another, listening, staring, commenting among themselves.

"I suppose you're glad to be sold, Olive," said Toaquin, sitting down carefully, as a grown Apache woman should.

"It really doesn't matter to us," said Olive after a moment. She had learned that she must choose her words carefully. Of all the Apaches, she hated Toaquin most. She was the one who seemed to take the greatest delight in making their lives unbearable. But Olive was afraid of her, too. Silence and obedience, that was the safest way to deal with Toaquin.

"I'm sorry to see you go. I had hoped to set you free in a short time, but now it will never happen." Olive knew Toaquin's words were false, so she said nothing. But Mary was not so discerning.

"Free?" she repeated. She would have said more, but in the darkness Olive pinched her arm. The pinch said that Toaquin was lying. She often lied, just to make them unhappy or to get them into trouble.

"There was talk," Toaquin assured them carelessly. "But when the Mohaves offered to buy you, we could hardly refuse. They're trading two horses and three blankets and some beads and vegetables. Far more than you are worth. So naturally the Smart One and my father said yes."

She waited a minute, but when they didn't answer, she went on.

"I hate to see you go with the Mohaves, Olive. They are very cruel. They steal and lie and cheat. I suppose you think they will let you go sometime?"

"No," said Olive quietly.

"Well, they won't," Toaquin told her viciously. "When they're tired of you, they'll sell you to another tribe. Someone even worse than they are."

"We are captives." Olive tried to keep the fear from her voice. What Toaquin said could very well be true.

"I hate the Mohaves," said Toaquin angrily. "I wish they'd never come here to trade. There's something strange about them. Something that isn't right. Why should their chief send his daughter, a girl, to decide whether or not you were worth trading for? No Apache would do a thing like that."

"Perhaps it was because she speaks your language," suggested Mary timidly. "Or maybe because he loves her."

"Those are stupid reasons." Toaquin sprang to her feet, glaring down at them. "No, it must be because, as a woman, she can judge how much work you'll be able to do. If you think you worked hard for us, wait till you see what the Mohaves

71

expect of you. And another thing. It's nine days' journey to their country, not four, as when you came here. And they cover great distances each day. Don't think the Mohaves will carry you, Mary. Not the way the Apaches did. And when you get there, don't pretend to be filled with the devils of sickness. The Mohaves will not take care of you, as we did. They will let you die."

Olive had never seen anyone so angry. Even in the shadows she could see that Toaquin's brown face was flushed. Her skin looked drawn and taut, and her eyes were narrow slits. She glared at them both a moment, but before she turned to go she had one thing more to say.

"Olive! Olive! Olive!" she screamed as loudly as she could. "Mary! Mary! Olive! Mary!"

Chapter 6

TOPEKA WAS WORRIED. HAD SHE MADE A mistake in trading for the two slaves? In the beginning she had mentioned how their bones protruded from their skin, but the Apaches had assured her such a thing was natural to the white race. Now she was not so sure. Perhaps she had traded her father's good horses and blankets, beads and vegetables for a pair of weaklings.

She and the five warriors who accompanied her on this trading mission had made the trip from the banks of the Colorado to the wintering place of the Tonto Apaches in nine days. By white man's reckoning that was 350 miles. But this was the eleventh day of the return, and they were not yet home. The slaves were walking more and more slowly, while the small one's progress was halted often by long fits of coughing.

Topeka considered asking one of the warriors to take Mary behind him on his pony. Then she decided against it. She knew the men grumbled at the confidence Chief Espaniol placed in his daughter. It was she who had made the final decision about trading for the slaves. To suggest now that one of them was not strong enough to walk would be a confession of error in Topeka's judgment. No, they would just have to stumble along.

"Are you all right?" she asked Olive, who was walking behind her, supporting her sister.

Olive wasted no breath on words. She merely nodded. Topeka continued on, reassured. At least there had been no coughing spells for some time.

The five warriors rode ponies. On a trading mission such as this, it would have been loss of face to do otherwise. As the daughter of a chief, Topeka could have ridden if she'd wanted to. She preferred to walk. Even on the way to make the trade, when there were two extra ponies, she had not ridden. All Mohaves liked to walk. Their deep chests were meant for breathing. If necessary, their long legs could cover fifty miles a day. They could go from sunup to sundown without stopping for food. But not with the white slaves along. The Mohaves had been forced to slow their normal speed, and Topeka knew it was galling for the men to do so.

At night, when she shared her blanket with the two girls, she had heard the warriors grumbling. Why did the good-for-nothing whites have to dig every root along the trail? Why were they always complaining about their sore feet? At their age, feet should be hard as leather. Already the party was slowed down. On their return they would be the laughingstock of the Mohaves.

Topeka wondered about some of these matters, too. On a journey, food was rationed by the individual. Before setting out, the Apaches had given everyone a hunk of meat. Instead of making theirs last, the slaves had devoured their portions in a single day. It was as though they had never eaten before. After that they dug every root they saw growing to supplement their share of the ground meal carried by the Mohaves and occasional game shot by the warriors.

While the Apaches had permitted the slaves to keep their worn tunics and skirts, they withheld the moccasins, which were still in good condition. Soon their feet were torn and bleeding, so Topeka found strips of leather to bind around them. The only leather available was the slaves' thin tunics. The girls had made a great fuss when Topeka began tearing them into strips. It took threatening gestures from the warriors before they agreed at all. Topeka thought they were very foolish, since it was their feet that needed protection not the upper parts of their bodies. But even with the foot bindings, the slaves could not keep up. Topeka was glad this was the last mountain to climb.

She was suddenly aware that the riders ahead had halted. There was no need, she thought irritably. She and the slaves would catch up eventually. Then she saw it was for another reason. They had reached the crest of the Black Mountain. Every Mohave who had been away paused at this place on his return. It was his first glimpse of the place he loved best of all—his home.

"Yokia," she cried, turning to the gasping girls behind her. "We are almost at my father's village."

She hurried up the last incline and stood beside the riders at the top. Below her lay a narrow valley, still verdantly green, not turning brown and yellow as the mountains they had passed through. There were trees, mostly cottonwoods, and she knew that the sun would be making a pattern of light and shade beneath the leaves. Sloping up from either side were gentle hills, and above them rose the high, sharp peaks of mountains. Against the blueness of the sky, their crests were as jagged as the streaks of forked lightning that lived within those stony crags. From this spot Topeka could not see the river, but she knew it was there, just behind the trees. And that gauzy streak of smoke, like a lost cloud that hovered above the ground, came from her own village.

"See," she cried, as the white girls staggered up the last ascent. "That's where I live. That's my home."

They stared in the direction of her pointing finger, and the younger slave said something in her own tongue.

"What did she say?" Topeka asked Olive, for Mary Ann had begun to cough again. She hoped she wouldn't keep coughing once they arrived. Perhaps it was the high mountain air that brought it on.

"She said it was a beautiful valley and she'd like to live there," translated Olive.

"She's going to," said Topeka, smiling. "The Mohaves are good people. They will be kind to you unless you try to run away. Then they will kill you."

The air grew warmer as they began their descent into the valley. The warmth was their first welcome home, thought Topeka. Most of their journey had been through the mountains. It had been cold, especially at night, and more than once she had grown angry, remembering the third rabbit hair blanket that the Apaches had demanded in trade. By Mohave standards, it was not a very good blanket, and she had brought it for the slaves to use at night. But the Tonto Apaches had no dealings with other tribes, and their only blankets were obtained in raids on the Navajos. They wanted it along with the two good ones, and Topeka had given in. Her own blanket had to cover three.

She almost forgot the two girls stumbling behind in the pleasure of her homecoming. Autumn was coming. She could smell it in the air. It was a good smell, a smell of warm earth, of harvested crops, and wood smoke. The birds knew it was coming. Overhead, they sang and twittered about it, deciding among themselves whether they should stay or leave for a new home. A squirrel scampered down a bush, one cheek bulging with a nut, which Mohave eyes had overlooked. Topeka smiled after it. The squirrel was welcome to the nut. It had been a good year, and she knew the storage bags hanging from the roof of her father's house were full.

Within a few hours they reached the outskirts of the village. People came running from their houses to stand before the outer enclosure and call and wave to Topeka and the warriors as they passed.

Topeka glanced over her shoulder at the slaves, hoping they would notice how much better the Mohaves lived than the Tonto Apaches. Each dwelling was surrounded by a fence of cut poles, enclosing a garden patch. And within the garden was a thatched dwelling, also built of sturdy poles. It was a permanent village, not a camp to be moved with the seasons. When she saw the slaves were too tired to lift their eyes from the dust, she tried to stifle her disappointment. Tomorrow when they were rested, they would see and realize how lucky they were.

Then the river came into view, and Topeka momentarily forgot everything else. The river was life to the Mohave. Every year, or almost every year, it overflowed its banks, and when it receded, the fresh brown silt grew wondrous crops, wheat and corn, beans and melons. All that was expected of the Mohave was that he dig a hole, insert the seed, and the sun and the river did the rest. Of course, there was never quite enough to last until the next harvest, but supplemented with wild fruits and seeds, it was a blessing given to no other people. When the river receded, it sometimes left small lakes or ponds containing fish, and there were certain tribesmen who were lucky with traps and could snare fish from the very river itself.

Topeka said her greetings to the river, breathing in its special fragrance, before she turned up the slight elevation that led to her father's house.

Chief Espaniol and his wife Vimaka awaited their arrival at the doorway of the outer enclosure. Topeka's heart filled with love at seeing them. How handsome they were! Her father was tall, one of the tallest in a tribe known for its great height. And if there were threads of gray in the black hair that hung loose about his shoulders, his face was unlined with age. It was a broad face, an intelligent face, and in addition to the special lines of blue tattooing on his chin, there was also a blue circle tattooed on his forehead. He wore a new breechcloth, one that Topeka had never seen, and handsome fringed moccasins.

Her mother was shorter and beautifully plump. The brown legs beneath the shredded bark skirt were dimpled and there were dimples in her elbows. Two strings of blue beads hung from her neck against her bare bosom. Her hair was cut square across her eyebrows, and today she had plaited the back portion tightly and coated it with something sticky. Lice again, thought Topeka sympathetically. Some people simply ignored lice in their hair, but not Vimaka. She always took immediate steps to get rid of them. Her eyes were soft and brown, and the full mouth, above the tattooed chin, was smiling warmly.

"Welcome, daughter," said Espaniol. "Welcome home."

"We missed you," said her mother. "The days seemed long. Come in."

"I'm sorry we are late," Topeka told them. "The slaves were not able to keep up. They slowed us down."

"Who can keep up on the trail with a Mohave?"

asked Espaniol proudly. "It is no matter. The important thing is that you are home."

Topeka motioned the girls to follow, and with her parents, she entered the gate. The garden patch was already harvested, she observed, as they passed through and into the house. This was always the last. Because of its proximity to the house, it had more protection. The gardens by the river had to be watched carefully and gathered the moment produce was ripe. Even in so well run a village as her father's, there was danger of thieves.

The single room was hot, and she could see it was because coals were glowing in the special place beside the door where the fire was always laid.

"We didn't know when you would arrive," explained her mother. "But I knew you would be hungry when you got here. See, there's a corn cake in the ashes to hold you until I can prepare a meal."

With an exclamation of delight, Topeka leaned down and snatched the corn cake. It was hot, but not hot enough to burn. She broke it into three pieces and handed a section to Mary, another to Olive.

"It is good to be home," she said, biting into her own portion happily.

Chapter 7

BOTH OLIVE AND MARY HAD BEEN ENCOUR-
aged by Topeka's kindness. They hoped
life with the Mohaves would be easier than
it had been with the Tonto Apaches. Aside from
the fact that they were now rid of Toaquin's constant supervision, there was little change. They
were still slaves, and as slaves they were expected
to work constantly for their master.

Sometimes Olive wondered if she and Mary Ann
would have to spend the rest of their lives as slaves.
Back home she had never thought much about

slavery. She knew it existed in other states, of course, and there had even been times when she thought wistfully of how nice it would be to have a slave to do her work. She didn't think so now.

But at least they could talk with Topeka in a way that had been impossible with Toaquin. Topeka was always willing to answer questions, and she even volunteered information. She told them that, beyond those jagged mountains to the west, there were other white men. They lived in the land belonging to the Yumas. And since the Yumas were friends, the Mohaves sometimes received articles in trade that had come from the whites, beads and red flannel and pieces of iron. Topeka always concluded with the warning of what would happen to a slave who attempted to escape, but Olive didn't believe that part. A slave was a valuable possession. It would be foolish to kill a slave who was still able to work.

As the winter passed, she often looked at the rough peaks, now white with snow, and wished that she were a bird. But even with only two feet, escape might not be impossible. All a body had to do was walk to the top, then walk down the other side. It couldn't be that hard. A Yuma runner had arrived in camp one day, and she had asked Topeka how long he had been on the trail. She was greatly encouraged to hear that it had been only two days. Two days was even less than she had figured. Mary Ann could certainly walk that distance. She had withstood the long journey from the Apache camp better than Olive thought she could.

There was still that uncontrollable cough, however. Suppose they were in hiding and Mary Ann was taken by a seizure? The cough would give them away to any nearby Mohave tracker. But surely the cough would go away when the sun grew hot. And they couldn't leave now, anyway, not with snow still in the mountains.

"But soon we'll get away," she assured Mary Ann, staring hard at the white-tipped barrier. "Some day we'll be living with our own people again."

"It's going to feel funny living with the whites," said Mary Ann, making her sister's heart turn over in alarm. "Running Deer was nice, but I like the Mohaves better. Especially Vimaka and Topeka."

"But they're so dirty," Olive reminded her quickly. She mustn't let Mary Ann get attached to these people and forget that she was white. "They're worse than the Apaches because they don't jump in the river every day. They only swim when they feel like it, and the river's so muddy it doesn't get them clean. Besides, they're ugly, with all that tattooing. And their children are so rude."

"The children were pretty mean at first," agreed Mary Ann. "But I think they're getting better."

On their arrival, the Mohave children had been especially hard to bear. Although Olive and Mary

Ann were the property of Chief Espaniol and lived in his house, it was soon apparent that they were expected to take orders from everyone in the tribe.

Each morning when the girls appeared, carrying baskets strapped on their backs, they were surrounded by a crowd of children, each with a demand for some service. Sometimes Vimaka had to intervene, reminding the children that the slaves must do her bidding first. She always did this with her pleasant smile and a promise that as soon as the slaves had carried enough wood or water or gathered sufficient wild food to serve her needs, she would send them out to the children.

The Mohaves ate better than the Apaches, but there was little game in their valley. Meat consisted mainly of small animals like rabbits and squirrels, and while it was not denied young girls, there was only a little left over by the time the family had eaten its fill. There was sometimes fish from the muddy Colorado. The flesh was soft and there were many bones—"scrap fish," Olive called it scornfully—but everyone devoured it with great relish.

Snow lingered on the mountain crests long after spring arrived in the valley. The Mohaves pointed with pride to green plots of winter wheat that had been sowed last fall, but to Olive it looked a little strange, for it grew in hills rather than in rolling fields. Soon, they said, it would be time to plant corn and beans and pumpkin. Right now their staple food was dried mesquite beans, which Vimaka had hung in bags from the thatched roof of her house, and roots.

One morning Olive awoke to find unusual excitement in the household. Usually the slaves were up first, but today Vimaka must have forgotten to awaken them. Both she and Espaniol were dressing in what they considered their best clothes and smearing their faces with lines and slashes of red and black paint. There were six strings of white and blue beads around Vimaka's dirty, plump neck today, instead of two, but Espaniol still wore only his breechcloth.

"No one woke us," said Olive to Topeka, who was standing, smiling approval at her parents. "Does your mother want wood, or shall we dig roots this morning?"

Instead of answering, Topeka spoke rapidly to her father in their own tongue. She was one of the few members of the tribe who spoke Apache, and since it pleased her to act as interpreter, the girls had been slow in learning the Mohave language. It was almost as if Topeka didn't want them to learn, as though she wanted to keep them for herself. However, they were learning anyway and could follow a conversation when someone spoke slowly.

"My father says you may delay your work to watch the beginning of the planting," Topeka reported finally. "He says it is fitting that his slaves see how their master attends to the welfare of his family."

"Planting?" repeated Olive stupidly.

"Kitkilha, our wise shaman, says this is the proper day to place the seeds in the breast of the earth mother. He had it in a dream. Soon the seeds will grow into sturdy plants, and the plants will yield corn and beans and melons for the Mohave."

"We've seen planting before," began Mary Ann, but Olive nudged her into silence.

"It's better than digging roots," she whispered.

The river's bank, where during the winter months the Colorado raced, gray and swollen, had changed since they saw it yesterday. The soft mud, cracking a little under the spring sun, was now dotted with upright branches of small trees and bushes. They were spaced some distance apart, and each was marked by some object, a special feather, a bead, a wisp of red flannel, or the claw of a bird. These, Topeka explained, were identifying marks of the owner. Each household had an individual plot of ground. It was theirs to plant and harvest in addition to the small garden space within their fenced enclosures.

Apparently the planting was all done by men, and Olive decided it must have some religious significance, for one of the shamen, his face covered with a mask, did one of those special dances that always seemed to her to be nothing more than jumping up and down and waving his hands. As he danced, he sang one of his tuneless songs.

While they were waiting for the shaman to finish, Olive had an uncomfortable feeling that someone was staring at her. When she looked over at the group of bystanders, she saw that a young man, perhaps Topeka's age, was regarding her with open curiosity. She felt her face grow warm with shame and turned her back. She would never get used to wearing only a petticoat of shredded bark with the upper part of her body fully exposed. She didn't care if all the women dressed that way. She didn't feel decent.

Vimaka had presented petticoats to both her and Mary Ann soon after they arrived. They had been forced to put them on. Then Espaniol, Vimaka, and Topeka had smiled and stared and chattered in Mohave. Olive was glad that Ma didn't know how scandalously her two daughters were clad.

When the shaman finished, the chief of the Mohaves led off the planting. His was the plot marked by the strip of red flannel, and he stooped down and inserted his forefinger as far as it would go into the mud. Then, from a bag he carried, he pulled out a few seeds, dropped them in the hole and pushed the soft mud over the top.

"Ah!" said all the Mohaves, in a great sigh of appreciation. The first seeds for the next harvest had just been planted.

"Don't they plow the ground?" asked Olive in surprise.

Topeka stared vacantly. The word "plow" had, from necessity, been in English, and she didn't know what it meant.

Espaniol took a long stride over the soft ground, then once again repeated the process of planting a new hill of seeds. Soon all the men were following his example, sowing their individual plots. The shaman, meanwhile, continued dancing in small circles and chanting.

"Let's go," whispered Mary Ann. "I'm hungry, and probably breakfast won't be for hours."

Topeka seemed surprised that they did not want to watch the conclusion of the planting ceremony, but she gave her permission.

"Just so long as you don't try to run away," she added. Every day she warned them of this. "They'll kill you if you do."

"I don't see how they can be so sure they'd catch us if we did run away," said Mary Ann resentfully, as they walked away. "You said it wasn't too far to Fort Yuma. They walk there all the time."

"We don't know the trail and they do," Olive reminded her. "But maybe it will be sooner than you think." She looked at her little sister speculatively. Mary Ann had only coughed twice that morning. Maybe she was getting better.

Roots were not hard to find, for at this season

the green stems and leaves betrayed the bulb beneath the surface. There were some closer at hand, but the girls walked a distance up the hill to get away from the Mohaves on the riverbank. Even at this distance, the sound of the shaman's chanting was carried by the clear, clean air.

"That's not much of a song," said Mary Ann disdainfully, thrusting her digging stick into the soft ground. "It's only got two or three notes."

"They probably never heard a real song," said Olive sensibly. But she agreed the chant was not melodious. It went on and on, repeating the same notes without variation. "Let's us sing something," she suggested impulsively.

"Sing?" repeated Mary Ann in a puzzled voice. "What would we sing? I don't remember the words to a whole song."

Olive felt a great surge of remorse. She had neglected her duty. As the elder, she had done her best to protect her little sister, always hurrying to fill her own basket so she could help fill Mary Ann's. She had worried about her health, made sure she ate all her food, however tasteless, and reminded her to say her prayers each night. But there were other things that mattered, little things that linked them to the home Mary Ann must not forget. Singing was one of them.

The girls had not sung since the night the Tonto Apaches had come walking into camp, leaving death and devastation. But before that, the

Oatman family had sung a great deal. Ma had a clear, high soprano and Pa was a baritone. All the children could carry a tune, and they had sung together back home in Illinois and all the way from Independence to New Mexico. Somebody was forever starting a tune, then the others would join in one by one until everyone was singing. It made those bumpy, monotonous miles easier to bear.

"Do you remember this?" she asked, and began one of the hymns that they had sung each Sunday in church.

"The spirit of God, like a fire is burning!
The latter-day glory begins to come forth;
The visions and blessings of old are
    returning;
The angels are coming to visit the earth."

After the first moment of surprise, Mary Ann smiled and joined in. She had a high, sweet voice like Ma's, and together they finished all the verses. After that Olive began another song.

It was strange how singing made their work easier. The roots almost dug themselves, and the heap of white and brown tubers grew higher and higher in the baskets. One of the reasons, Olive told herself, was that if you were singing you couldn't eat at the same time. They might be sorry later on if the chief's family devoured all the breakfast and there were no leavings.

She was suddenly aware, as she had been at the

planting ground, that someone was staring at her. Looking over her shoulder, she saw that the whole tribe had left the river's edge, ascended the slope, and were now standing some few yards away. Mary Ann saw the audience at the same time, and the song ended abruptly.

"What sounds are you making?" asked Topeka after a moment.

"We're singing," explained Olive guiltily. The Mohaves looked very grave. No one was smiling.

"Is it a curse to make the seeds rot in the ground?" demanded Topeka fearfully.

"Oh, no! It's just a song. A song to God, praising Him and thanking Him for His goodness."

When Topeka translated, all the Mohaves seemed relieved.

"We have heard of your God," reported Topeka. "Black robes came among our people once and told us something of him. He does not seem a very strong god. He let himself be killed by men."

"But that was a sacrifice. It was to save us. To save all men."

"It did not save you," Topeka reminded her gently. "You are still a slave. Are you sure the songs are not harmful?"

"No," Olive assured her earnestly. "They are only good."

"Then my father says you may sing more of your songs," reported Topeka finally. "The Mohaves will listen."

For fifteen minutes more the girls sang hymns while the Indians listened wide-eyed and attentive. Finally Mary Ann's voice broke, and she began to cough.

"We can't sing anymore today," said Olive, hoping they would accept the decision. Mary Ann was almost doubled up by her coughing. "We've sung all we know. Maybe another day."

Topeka's dark eyes took in the situation intelligently. What she said to her people, Olive didn't know, but they seemed to accept the fact that the singing was at an end. They began wandering down the slope, back to their garden patches.

Only one stayed behind, the young man who had stared at Olive during the planting ceremony. She tried to ignore him, turning her bare back and plunging her digging stick viciously into the ground.

She was always uncomfortable when Mohave men glanced in her direction. Part of it was shame for her uncovered breasts, but there was another fear. What if one of them should lay his hands upon her? Dirty, heathen savages, she thought, shuddering. She would kill herself before she let that happen. Killing oneself was a sin, but it was a lesser sin than that thing often warned against from the pulpit.

"I would speak with you," the young man said in the Apache tongue. "I am Cearekae."

"I can't talk to you," Olive told him, bending

low over the ground and being careful to keep her back turned. She motioned Mary Ann to return to her digging. Her little sister had turned to inspect the man curiously. Of course, Mary Ann was still young. Her chest was as flat as a boy's, and she seemed to have no sense of shame. Olive told herself she would have to have a talk with Mary Ann about decency and public exposure.

"Go away," she said to the young man. "We are slaves. We have work to do. We can't talk to you."

"We will speak later," said Cearekae after a moment.

When she finally found the courage to lift her head, he was gone.

Chapter 8

TOPEKA WAS MAKING A NEW KRAOKI FOR HER mother. She sat before the doorway of her father's house, a heap of yellow clay beside her on the ground and the half-finished bowl on her thigh. With the palms of her hands, she rolled the clay to a thin string, then twisted the string around and around, patting it carefully so there would be no holes or crevices in the finished *kraoki* after it had been burned in the fire.

Among the Mohaves, Topeka was known as a

maker of fine pottery. She also excelled in all household tasks. She was strong, and Espaniol often boasted of her intelligence. Hadn't she learned the language of the Apache? It was an accomplishment that not many of the Mohaves had bothered to attain. She could be trusted, as in the case of trading for the white slaves, to act for her father, to use the same judgment that he himself would exercise. She was not unattractive, nor was her tongue the kind that slits another's feelings with its edge. Why then, she wondered, when other girls two years younger than herself were finding husbands, was she still unwed?

Topeka thought of this thing while she sat in the morning sunshine, her hands busy with the yellow clay.

There had been offers, of course, but each time Espaniol had turned the suitor down, declaring him unworthy. Topeka wasn't sure that this was so in every case. There had been brave warriors among them and sons of rich men.

It was true there had not been one who caused the blood to rush to her cheeks or made her breathe a little faster. Had that been so, she might have protested the dismissal, and her father would have given in. He had never denied her anything. As it was, she was content to abide by Espaniol's decision. But sometimes, as now, she wondered if there was something wrong with her. It was past time for marriage, yet here she was living in her father's house while all her friends were making homes of their own.

Espaniol and Vimaka were not anxious to have her leave. Topeka was their only child. If she married, she would have to move away. She could not bring her husband here to live since it was forbidden for mother-in-law and son-in-law to look each other in the face. They had been very close, the three of them, and marriage would break that intimacy. But it would have to come sometime, thought Topeka. Here she was, a woman of seventeen summers. By now she should have a husband and babies of her own.

A shadow fell across the sunlight at her feet, and Topeka looked up, startled. It was Cearekae, a young man of the tribe close to her own age. They had played together as small children, but of course that was long ago.

Cearekae was tall, almost as tall as her father, with a deep chest and wide shoulders. He was too young to be distinguished as a warrior, but his broad face was intelligent. He often served as one of the *g'an* dancers for the shaman, and it was said that his dreams were good.

"I have come to the daughter of our chief to ask her help," said Cearekae uncomfortably. Young men did not often seek out young women in this way.

Topeka nodded without speaking. For some reason, she too was uncomfortable.

97

"I have been trying to talk with the slaves, the *hiccos*." Cearekae used the Mohave word meaning "thieving whites," and by his tone Topeka knew he did not approve of them. "They will not talk to me. I beg the daughter of the chief to order them to do so."

"Why do you want them to talk with you?" she asked in bewilderment.

"Because I wish to learn their language," explained Cearekae. He was careful not to look at her directly, since that would have been rude. "I have learned the tongue of the Apache. Now I wish to learn that of the *hicco*. More and more of them are coming into our country. When they speak among themselves, it would be useful to know what they say, especially if they did not know I understood."

"That is very clever of you." Topeka let herself glance at Cearekae quickly before she looked away. The small boy she had once played with had grown into a young man of intelligence, she told herself.

"Will you help me?" he asked earnestly.

"Of course, I will," she agreed. "The slaves are gathering the seeds of the *akatai* so my mother may store them for the cold time. We will go there at once."

"If the daughter of the chief will go first," suggested Cearekae humbly, "I will follow at a distance."

Topeka covered her bowl and clay with wet leaves so they would not dry and got to her feet. Truly, this was a very superior young man. Not only was he intelligent, but he was also courteous.

Olive and Mary had climbed the hill a little way from the village where the *akatai* bushes dotted the slope. The seeds grew ready for harvesting at the same time the pumpkin and melons were ripening beside the river. For that reason, some of the Mohaves neglected to harvest the wild seeds. What was the use, they asked, when their houses were full of bounty from the planting?

But Vimaka knew that if they waited the birds would strip the bushes. Besides, she had two slaves to do her work. Baskets of *akatai* and *aksanta* seeds hung from the ceiling of her household, as well as bags of mesquite beans, awaiting the time when the vegetables were eaten.

Topeka walked up to the girls and smiled when they looked at her questioningly. No, she had not come to take them from their task. They were to continue picking while they talked.

When Cearekae arrived, she was surprised to see Olive glance at him with fear and deliberately turn her back. What was she afraid of? Such a handsome young man, too!

"Cearekae wishes you to teach him the language of the whites. And to know more of their customs."

"Must I?" Olive's voice was very small.

"You see?" said Cearekae. "It is as I said. She will not talk to me."

"Yes," said Topeka severely. "You must." She could not understand what had gotten into the slave. Usually Olive was very docile. "Cearekae speaks Apache, so you may use that language."

"Do you like living with the Mohaves?" asked Cearekae politely.

"I do not like it as well as living with the whites. You do not have enough here to eat," replied Olive after a moment. Her voice was muffled, for she did not turn around.

"We have enough to satisfy us," Cearekae told her, frowning. "Your people work hard, and it does you no good. We enjoy ourselves."

"'We enjoy ourselves at home." Olive's voice was a little louder now. "And our hard work does do good. We have more food and better houses and all sorts of things that you don't have."

Topeka's face grew serious. That was no tone for a slave to use when speaking to a young Mohave warrior. She would have reproved Olive herself, but Cearekae spoke first.

"Our grandfathers worked just as you whites do, and they had nice things to wear and eat. But the floods came and swept the old people away, and a son of the family stole all the animals and clothing. He left the Mohave with nothing."

"That's ridiculous!" Olive swung around angrily, then just as quickly faced the bush again.

For a moment Topeka thought that Cearekae was about to strike the slave. And rightly so. His face was filled with anger, and the muscles in his arms swelled with tightness. But instead he stayed where he was, and when he spoke, his voice was cold and contained.

"I will tell you how it happened," he said carefully, and Topeka held her breath, knowing that he was speaking of the great Mohave dream, which came only to those who were blessed. "Once all the people in the world were one family. They had great riches, clothing, cattle, horses, much to eat. Then came a great flood, and the members of this family took refuge on that mountain behind which the sun arises every morning. The flood covered all the world, and everything but the family and its possessions were destroyed, for the top of the mountain remained above the water. When the flood subsided, one of the family stole all the cattle and clothing and went toward the home of the winter winds. There his skin was changed from red to white, and his name became *Hicco,* which means 'thieving white.' Another member of the family took all the deerskins and bark, and from his loins sprang all the tribes of Indians. The *hiccos* will lose their cattle and riches yet, for the thieves will someday turn upon themselves."

"Olive," said the younger slave, when Cearekae stopped speaking. "That sounds like Noah and the ark, doesn't it?"

"Not a bit," denied her sister quickly. "It isn't nice to say that, either. Noah is from the Bible. This is just heathen superstition."

Cearekae gave no sign that he had heard. He continued speaking in the voice of one who interprets dreams.

"The mountain is called Hippoweka, which means 'spirit,' " he said reverently. "No one may climb its slopes, for if the feet of man should walk there, a great fire would burst forth and instantly consume him. At the top is a big house where the ancient family once lived, and there are still remnants of articles there that were used by them."

"How do you know if no one can walk there?" asked Mary curiously.

"Hush," said Topeka quickly. It was not wise to interrupt one who was speaking of these things.

"On the slopes of Hippoweka abide the spirits of every *hicco* ever killed by a Mohave. The *hicco* spirits are bound by chains and must ever endure the unquenchable fires from within the mountain," concluded Cearekae, his voice taking on a pleased note. "And to the Mohave who slew him goes eternal honor and tribal privileges."

"And those eternal fires sound like—" began Mary, but this time it was Olive's turn to say, "Hush."

Cearekae heard her. He turned to stare at each of the two white slaves in turn. There was hatred in his black eyes, and Olive moved closer to her little sister as though to offer her own body as protection. But Cearekae did not raise his hand against them, he only glared. After a time he shrugged and seemed to dismiss them from his mind.

"It was a poor idea after all," he told Topeka. "I would be wasting my time to learn the language of the *hiccos*. For these bad people will soon kill each other anyway." He turned and stalked down the slope, his head high, the apron flaps of his breechcloth switching disdainfully.

Topeka looked after him in admiration. She had never met a young man who impressed her so much. Certainly, Cearekae was destined for great things. Then she turned to the slaves with disapproval.

"You were rude," she accused. "You have shamed me. I should order you to be beaten."

"I'm sorry," said Olive stubbornly. "I don't like that man. He keeps watching me. I've seen him. It's been going on for months."

"Why should he not watch you if he likes?" demanded Topeka. "It is not as though you were a Mohave maiden. You are only a slave."

"But what if he should put his hands on me or try to touch me? Ma always warned me about strange men."

Suddenly Topeka understood.

"The Mohaves do not take a girl against her will, nor do the Apaches," she said pityingly. "It

103

is only your people and the Mexicans who do that. The Mohave would not stoop so low. If you found a Mohave brave you liked and he liked you, he might make you his wife. But it would only be with your consent."

"Oh," said Olive weakly.

"And Cearekae would never want you for a wife." Surprisingly, Topeka found herself growing angry. "He is a fine young man and intelligent. He has no use for *hiccos*."

Chapter 9

OLIVE WAS SURPRISED AT HARVEST TIME. The crops had been given little care. No one bothered to hoe or weed, and even watering was a spasmodic affair, done when the owner remembered. But still there was a goodly amount of corn and beans, pumpkin and melons.

There was constant work for the slaves to do, for wild plants must be harvested and stored in bags and baskets. By evening, Mary Ann was so exhausted that she could only lie in her corner of the chief's house and sleep. Any plans for running away had to be postponed until she was stronger.

Almost before they knew it, autumn was there again, and after that came winter. Again there was snow in the high mountains surrounding the valley, but although the nights were cold the days were bearable. Some of the Mohaves put on robes of woven rabbit hair, but the slaves were expected to make do with their petticoats of shredded bark. The chill came on gradually, and Olive did not notice it as much as she had the first winter. But she did wish that Mary Ann had been given warmer garments. A person with a cough should be well wrapped up, maybe with a flannel bib to protect her chest. At least, they both had the protection of the chief's roof every night.

Olive had hardened in other ways as well. She no longer felt the need to cover her breasts with her arms as she had done before. After all, these were only savages. They knew no better. To them a bare breast had no more significance than an uncovered face. Probably the heathen women in a faraway country she had heard about would be horrified to have their veils taken from their faces.

Cearekae had long ago stopped staring at her when they met, and the matter of English lessons had never been referred to again. Sometimes Olive felt a little foolish when she remembered how frightened she had been. But it was only natural. Ma had warned her against men and sin, and when a man stared at you every time you met, what was a body to think? If only Topeka had explained things to her before, she might have acted differently. She wouldn't mind teaching English to any Mohave who wanted to learn. Pa always said learning was a good thing, and Olive had never been one to shirk her duty. She would have explained all this to Topeka if she had dared, but for weeks after the incident on the hillside Topeka had been cool to her. Olive was afraid to bring it up later for fear the coolness would return.

Often, when there were guests, Olive and Mary Ann were called upon for entertainment, and the Indians listened attentively while they went through church hymns and childish songs they remembered from home. Sometimes the visitors rewarded them with a bead or two. By now each had a small string of beads to hang around her neck, and once Espaniol had given them a small strip of red flannel. It was not big enough to serve as a garment, but they put it away carefully. Perhaps sometime they would receive more to add to it. If only they could collect enough cloth to make themselves shirts, Olive felt she might feel decent again. But she resolved the first shirt should go to Mary Ann. It might give her a little protection when the cold winds blew off the mountains, making her cough on and on.

One morning, when the winter was once more behind them and the river had receded from its annual overflow, Vimaka gave Olive a small handful of seeds.

"The chief says I may give you these," she explained. "You talk about how much better the white man sows his crops. This is your chance to prove it. The chief has allotted a space of ground for your own use."

Olive stared at the seeds in her palm, hardly able to believe her good fortune. She looked at Vimaka happily, wondering how to say her thanks. By now she had learned much of the Mohave language, but so far as she knew there was no word for "thank you."

"My heart is very full," she said, and Vimaka seemed satisfied.

"If only we had a plow," she said to Mary Ann helplessly.

"Maybe we could turn the ground over with sticks," suggested Mary Ann. "If we don't do that, we'll just have to put the seeds in holes the way the Mohaves do."

"We'll use sticks," decided Olive. "We'll turn it as deep as we can."

Whenever they found a moment free from their daily tasks, they worked on the small plot of ground, turning the river soil as deeply as they could. The Mohaves watched with interest and ribald comments, which the girls did their best to ignore. They marked off rows for the beans and corn and planted the few pumpkin seeds in hills.

"We must carry water every day from the river," insisted Olive. "We've got to show them. After all our talk, it would be terrible if nothing came up."

But by this time the Mohaves had something else to occupy their attention. It had been decided to make war against the Cochapas, a large tribe several hundred miles away, with whom the Mohaves had never been at peace. Sixty warriors had been chosen to make up the expedition, and to Olive's satisfaction Cearekae was one of them. She had taken an active dislike to him in spite of Topeka's assurance he meant her no physical harm.

All day the men sat about preparing their weapons, their willow bows, almost the height of a man, and their feathered arrows made of arrow weed, their mallet-headed clubs of mesquite wood, and for fighting at close quarters, their *tokyetas*, straight sticks of heavy mesquite.

The women were opposed to the expedition, and because, in the Mohave tribe, they were given freedom to scold, they exercised that privilege. From morning until night they did their best to persuade the men to stay at home. The whole thing was foolish, they said. It was merely a lust for battle. There were rumors that the Cochapas had increased in strength. What if they should all be killed?

Olive listened indifferently. She didn't care whether the Mohave engaged in war or not. It was nothing to her if they were all killed, their bodies left forgotten in some distant country. It would serve them right.

She wondered, not for the first time, if some passing emigrant train had found the wreckage of the Oatman wagon and had given her family a Christian burial. She prayed for it every night. It would be terrible if Ma and Pa and her sisters and brothers had just lain there all this time, exposed to wild animals and all kinds of weather. But even if they had been found, strangers would not know that there had been two more in the family. They would never dream that she and Mary Ann had been taken captive. No one would ever think to look for them.

On the night before their departure, there was a celebration in honor of the warriors. The shaman chanted and the people danced. As usual, Mary Ann was tired, so Olive stayed with her in Espaniol's deserted house. Vimaka had prepared no evening meal, since there would be food at the celebration, and the girls ate a supper of cold roots and piñon nuts. Mary Ann fell asleep almost immediately, but Olive stayed awake a long while, listening to the pounding drums and the voices outside.

At dawn the war party started out. Each man carried a gourd of water, another of wheat, and his weapons. Their faces were painted with red and yellow clay, and they left on foot.

"Why don't they take the horses?" Olive asked Topeka, who was watching the departure from her father's doorway. "It's a long way, isn't it?"

"The horses might be killed. It is better to go on foot." There was something in Topeka's voice that made Olive look at her sharply. It was the same tone her sister Lucy had used when she said good-bye to her young man back home in Illinois.

"You don't want them to go?" she asked.

Topeka shook her head.

"It's because of Cearekae, isn't it?" asked Olive shrewdly. She remembered how angry Topeka had been on the hillside and her coolness afterward. She had never seen the two together since, but she wasn't sure how these matters were arranged among heathens. It wasn't like back home where a young man could walk a girl home from church.

"It's his first battle," said Topeka after a moment.

"And I'm sure he'll do very well," insisted Olive. She was a little surprised to hear herself. She sounded just like Ma, trying to reassure one of the children not to be afraid of the dark. "You'll be proud of him when he comes back."

Topeka looked at her and smiled.

"You are a good girl, Olive," she said. "What you say is true, but hearing you say it makes me feel better. I am glad my father bought you from the Apaches. You have served us well. I am going to speak to him about a reward."

It was three days before Olive discovered the nature of the reward. She and Mary Ann were preparing to set out for their morning's chores when Topeka stopped them.

"Not now," she said. "Not until later. Someone is coming."

"To see us? Do we have to sing?" asked Mary Ann anxiously. Her cough was always worse in the morning.

"No singing," Vimaka answered happily. "You will see."

Before long Kitkilha appeared in the doorway of Espaniol's house. Kitkilha was one of the Mohave shamen, and neither Olive nor Mary Ann had seen him so close at hand. Usually, as befitting his rank, he stayed apart from ordinary people, sitting in the sunny doorway of his house. He always seemed to be dozing, but Topeka said he was dreaming one of those magical dreams that made him a spiritual person.

Today, if he were dreaming, it must be a nightmare. His wrinkled face was twisted in a scowl, and he plopped the basket he was carrying on the earth floor with a vicious thump.

"I do not like this," he announced angrily. "And I will say no sacred words while I am working. Such a thing is not proper for common slaves."

"These are special slaves," Vimaka told him

112

coaxingly. "They are almost like my own daughters."

"I am here to obey the orders of the chief. I come for that reason only." Kitkilha scowled fiercely. "Tell the slaves to sit before me."

He lowered himself to the ground, and Topeka pushed Mary Ann and Olive down before them. He glared at them each in turn, then leaning over took a sharp pointed stick from his basket.

"Hold her head," he told Topeka gruffly. "I do not wish to soil my hands with a *hicco*."

Topeka stood behind Olive and held her head firmly with her two hands. The old man leaned forward, and she felt the tip of the sharp stick pricking her chin. Up and down it went, up and down. It didn't really hurt, not any more than a pinprick, and she sat quietly, wondering what it was all about. Some heathen custom, she supposed. When he had finished, he smeared something blue across her chin. A salve of some kind, she told herself, remembering how Ma had made special salves of goose grease. But why was he doing something to her chin? There was nothing wrong with it.

When he had finished with her, he repeated the process with Mary Ann.

"It is done," he said finally, struggling to his feet. "Say to the chief that Kitkilha has obeyed his orders."

"Let me see," cried Vimaka, as he stomped out through the door. "It is too soon to tell, but you will be beautiful. In the space of a few suns, you will hardly know yourselves."

"What is it? What did he do to us?" Mary Ann's eyes were watering. Her skin was more delicate than Olive's and the pointed stick had stung.

"He has tattooed your chins," said Topeka, laughing. "Didn't you know?"

"Tattooed our chins?" Olive wiped at the blue stuff, trying to rub it off. "Oh, how could you?"

"Because we are fond of you," said Vimaka, smiling. "And we want you to come to a good end when it is time. Everyone knows that the spirit of an untattooed person goes into a rat hole when he dies. We don't want that to happen to you."

"No," agreed Topeka. "If any warriors are killed in the battle against the Cochapas, your lives will be forfeit, since you are the only slaves in the village. It is always so. When a warrior dies in battle, his spirit goes south, to the land of melons and good things to eat. He will need a slave to serve him there. You will like that better than living in a rat hole, but it could not be before you were properly tattooed."

Olive stared at her in horror and disbelief. For a moment she could hardly comprehend this terrible thing that had been done to her and Mary Ann. Then, as she realized how they had been permanently marked, she did something she had not permitted herself to do since the night the Apaches had raided the Oatman wagon. She threw herself on the ground and cried as though her heart was broken.

Chapter 10

I T IS TOO BAD," SAID TOPEKA SYMPATHETICALLY. "But it is something that happens. It happens to other gardens, too, if they are not carefully guarded."

She stood with the white slaves looking at the row of corn, which only yesterday had been loaded with fat ears almost ripe enough for harvesting. Now the stalks were broken, and every ear was gone. During the night someone had stolen all the corn that Olive and Mary had planted and watered so carefully.

"But someone has it," Olive insisted. "If you'd look in all the houses, you'd find it."

Topeka shook her head. Such a thing was impossible. The missing corn would not be found in any house. By now whoever had taken it had hidden it carefully and would bring it out a little at a time to mix with his own harvest.

She was sorry for the slaves. They had worked hard on their little garden, but thievery was not unusual. The owner had to keep constant vigilance. A garden was a great worry. Mice or birds could eat the seeds before they sprouted, and once the corn was ripe, there was always the danger that it might be stolen. That was why second gardens were planted within the fenced enclosures of the houses. Thievery was more difficult there, although the location made the task of carrying water far more arduous.

"Your beans were good," she said, remembering how delicious they had tasted. Vimaka had cooked several pickings of beans, and the slaves had been given more than usual since it was they who were responsible. "And the pumpkins are ripening well."

Olive turned away without answering. Topeka turned, too, and immediately forgot about the stolen corn.

Coming down the hillside from the crest of the Black Mountain was a troop of small moving dots. There were too many to be a friendly trading

117

party. It was their own Mohave warriors, returning from their raid upon the Cochapas. Was Cearekae among them, Topeka wondered. And if so, had he conducted himself in a way to win honor?

Others had seen them, too, and cries and shouts were going up throughout the village. Women were rushing from their houses, children were jumping up and down and screaming, old men were hurrying for their paintpots that they might be suitably adorned to greet the returning warriors.

"Get wood," Topeka told Olive and Mary Ann quickly. "Much wood. There must be a big fire blazing when they arrive."

As they left to do her bidding, she looked after them. This might be the last order she would ever give them, for if Mohave braves had fallen in battle, the lives of the slaves must be sacrificed. But at least, Topeka told herself with satisfaction, if that happened, they need not spend eternity in a rat hole. Despite Kitkilha's reluctance, he had done a good job. The lines of blue tattooing running down Olive's and Mary Ann's chins were as fine as Topeka had ever seen.

She could not understand why, instead of being grateful, the slaves had cried. And Olive had actually shouted in a way no slave should ever do. She claimed the tattooing was a brand to let people know she belonged to the Mohaves; that it made her ugly and she wouldn't have it. Topeka had finally had to slap her a few times before she quieted down, and for days afterward she had been sulky. The *hiccos* were a strange people, Topeka told herself. Then her thoughts turned to practical matters, for there was much to do to make ready for the returning warriors.

By the time the war party reached the village, all was ready. The fire was blazing, with a pile of wet logs standing by in case smoke was needed for the purification ceremony of captives. Both men and women had painted their faces with red and yellow, according to their own distinctive designs. Strings of shells and beads were suspended around necks, and everyone lucky enough to own a bit of red flannel wore a band around his head.

Topeka, looking at her father's people, thought they would do honor to any returning war party. Then she noticed Olive and Mary standing very close to each other by the doorway of Espaniol's house. Waiting to see how many braves returned must be hard for them since their lives depended on it. But that was the way things were. They had always been so.

The warriors neared the village, and at once it was easy to see they had been victorious. Their heads were high, their eyes flashed, their steps were sure and firm. They did not look like men who had completed a walking journey of several hundred miles, and only a few had to be helped along by others. Topeka's eyes searched for and found Cearekae in the crowd, then modestly she looked away. But her heart was very full.

Sixty Mohave warriors had gone out. Sixty returned, although a few had suffered injuries. They had taken the Cochapas unawares, and it had been a great victory. The applause and shouts of those who awaited them rang across the river.

There was an additional cause for rejoicing. The Mohaves had captured five slaves. Four were girls between the ages of twelve and fifteen, but the fifth was a woman in her twenties.

When the people saw this, sticks of wet arrow-weed were thrown upon the fire. The smoke ceremony would be needed lest the captives bring sickness into camp. It had been a long time since Topeka had seen this ceremony. It had not been necessary to purify the white slaves, since they were purchased, not captured. And there would be another rite that must be observed now, also. The use of salt was prohibited for a full moon after the arrival of a captive. People were already complaining good-naturedly about it. Was a captive worth so many days of unsalted meat and fish?

Topeka was inclined to doubt it. The fish from the muddy Colorado was only palatable when liberally sprinkled with salt. Then she changed her mind.

The oldest captive belonged to Cearekae. It was his hand that thrust her into the purifying smoke and his voice that beseeched the gods to cleanse her of any sickness, lest she bring it to the Mohaves. Topeka watched proudly. The lack of salt was a small price to pay. The important thing was that Cearekae had won honor in his first battle.

Before many days had passed, it became clear that Cearekae's captive was not the prize everyone had thought. The four younger girls seemed reconciled to their lot. They obeyed orders, worked hard, brought credit to their masters, and began picking up a few words of the Mohave tongue. In time, they would all find husbands in the tribe.

Cearekae's slave, however, never stopped moaning and crying. Tears ran down her cheeks all the while her hands were gathering mesquite beans, and they mingled with the water that she carried from the river. No one could understand her strange words, since no one in the tribe spoke the Cochapa language, but Mary and Olive, with whom she was sent to work, reported that by means of signs she had told them her name was Nowerka and that she cried for a baby who had been taken from her.

Topeka was sorry about the baby, but she was relieved to see Nowerka cry so much. Men often married the slaves they took in battle, but Cearekae would never marry a continuous waterfall. And Topeka had decided that she would marry him herself. Girls usually married an older man, and she and Cearekae were of an age. It would cause talk, but that did not matter. When Cearekae had garnered a few more honors, she would speak to her father.

Then one morning, the village awoke to find Nowerka gone. She had disappeared during the night.

"She's run away," said Mary Ann enviously. "And I don't blame her. She wants her baby."

Topeka looked at her sadly. The small one understood so little.

"She will be caught and brought back," she said. "And when she is, she will die. I've warned you of such things many times. A slave is kindly treated unless she tries to run away."

"Maybe she won't be caught," suggested Olive.

"Oh, yes." Topeka was very sure. "Unless she has drowned herself in the river. Perhaps that is what happened."

Search parties went out for four days but were unsuccessful in picking up the trail. On the fifth day, a runner from the Yuma tribe arrived, driving Nowerka before him. He had found her hiding behind a rock, and since the Yumas and the Mohaves were friends, he was bound to return her to her owners.

The council sat in immediate judgment, and because Nowerka was Cearekae's slave, he was allowed to say by what means she must die. The elders were amazed at his decision. It was a manner unknown to them—a method by which Mohave prisoners had never been slain.

After the meeting they returned to their homes and reported the astonishing decision to their wives and families. Espaniol had just finished telling Vimaka and Topeka about it when Olive and Mary Ann arrived, carrying filled baskets of mesquite berries.

"They found her, didn't they?" asked Olive. "They found Nowerka?"

"They found her," agreed Espaniol, frowning. He still appeared shaken by the course Cearekae was taking.

"Are you going to kill her?" asked Mary Ann fearfully.

"Yes," said Topeka. At the horror she could read on the girl's face, she tried to soften the blow. "But she will die in the white man's way, not ours."

"Yes," agreed Espaniol. "Some of the men are lashing two tree trunks together now."

"I don't understand." Olive looked from one to another of the solemn brown faces.

"Cearekae spent some time in the Spanish mission near Yuma," explained Topeka, trying to keep her pride from showing. "They told him how the whites killed the son of your god. Nowerka will die in the same manner."

"You mean you're going to crucify her?" Olive gasped.

But no one answered. Mary Ann had suddenly fainted, and everyone was too concerned about her.

Chapter 11

AFTER NOWERKA'S DEATH, MARY ANN STOPPED talking of escape, and Olive tried not to remember that white men lived just beyond the mountains to the west. If a fate like that was the consequence of running away, it would be better to live out their lives in captivity.

The slaves had been forced to watch the crucifixion, and for weeks afterward Mary Ann awoke from sleep screaming. Olive always held her close, assuring her it was only a bad dream. But she knew better. She had seen it with her own eyes, and she would never forget that slim brown body fastened to the crossed tree trunks or her own relief when an arrow put an end to Nowerka's suffering.

The year that followed was the worst in the memory of the oldest Mohave. Winter snows had been scant in the mountains, and the Colorado did not overflow its banks. The drought continued into the spring, and the little rain that fell was not enough to sink deeply into the ground.

The tribesmen planted as usual in the parched riverbed and worried about the winter wheat that had been sown on higher ground last fall. It had come up late, and the stalks looked thin and spindly. At harvest time, the yield was next to nothing, and Chief Espaniol decreed that little should be saved for seed.

All summer the slaves, Mary Ann, Olive, and the four Cochapa girls, worked from dawn to dusk gathering what wild plants they could find. The Mohave women worked as tirelessly, but despite their efforts, there were few bags of mesquite beans and edible seeds hanging in the houses. There was little fish as well, for without the flooding river to create small ponds and pools, it was not easy to obtain.

Sickness was in the village, but the shaman insisted it was not caused by devils, but by hunger. Many of the tribesmen died, and one of the Cochapa slaves as well. Several times a week a funeral pyre blazed high, and the shrieks and cries of mourners continued far into the night.

Olive was frantic with worry about her sister. Mary Ann had always been thin, but now her skin covered only bones. Her cough was worse, and she was so weak she could hardly lift an empty *chiechuck*, the carrying basket woven of reeds and grasses. She never complained, but every day she spoke longingly of a bowl of bread and milk. Did Olive remember when they had their own cow? And when Ma baked bread? How good it smelled when it came fresh from the oven. Remember how she sometimes let them cut into a crusty loaf while it was still warm?

It hurt Olive to hear her talk like that, but in one way she was glad. At least Mary Ann hadn't forgotten everything about the past. She hadn't become an Indian.

By fall every edible root and plant within a day's distance of the village had been gathered. There was much rejoicing when a Yuma tribesman, calling on the Mohaves, spoke of a large tree he had seen in the mountains that was loaded with *oth-to-toa* berries. It was some sixty miles away, but that was of small matter. An expedition was organized immediately to go in search of it.

Olive knew that she would be expected to go, but Mary Ann would never be able to stand the trip. She spoke to Topeka about it, and the Indian girl's face grew serious.

126

"There will be much talk if she doesn't go," Topeka explained. "People will say that my father is growing soft. Mary is a slave, and slaves must work. The berries she could gather might mean life to some Mohave."

To Olive's surprise, Vimaka came to her support.

"The little one will not go," she said firmly. "She is too weak to walk to the nearest hillside. I know this place where they say the *oth-to-toa* grows. It is over steep mountains, and in places there is not even a trail. It will take great endurance to reach it, and the little one would soon be left behind. I will speak to the chief, and those who complain may do so to me."

Olive looked at her gratefully, and Topeka put a brown hand on her arm in sympathy.

"My mother will take care of your sister while we are gone. She will not let her starve. What she has, she will share with Mary."

Tears came to Olive's eyes, and she wiped them away quickly. Sometimes it was hard to remember Vimaka and Topeka were savages, for they had shown her only kindness. They even claimed that hideous tattooing on her chin had been ordered out of good will, but Olive would never believe that. She preferred to think it was a brand to mark her as the property of the tribe.

The party that set out was large, but many of those who usually picked berries were missing.

Like Mary Ann, they were too weak to bear burdens. A few braves accompanied the women, but they did not carry baskets strapped to their backs. Olive, plodding along with her *chiechuck* bouncing against her shoulders, looked at the men resentfully. Lazy louts! They're too proud to carry baskets, but they won't be too proud to eat the berries we pick. Her eyes passed over, without even seeing, the long bows and quivers filled with arrows carried by each warrior.

Vimaka had not been exaggerating when she said the way to the *oth-to-toa* was rugged. Olive had never climbed so tortuous a trail, and her empty basket grew heavier by the moment. Occasionally they found roots along the way, and the men shot a few birds and rabbits. When this happened, the slaves were given an equal share. They have to keep up our strength so we can work, thought Olive bitterly, gnawing on a blackbird's wing. Otherwise, they'd let us starve.

On the third day they reached the tree. It was more like a large bush than a tree, she decided, and resembled mesquite, although the leaves were bigger. It was covered with small berries that tasted a little like oranges. They would be good for Mary Ann. Perhaps they might take her mind for a little while from bread and milk.

"Is this the only bush around here?" she asked Topeka curiously. The pickers were making great headway with their work. Already the fruit was nearly gathered.

"Where there is one, there will be more," Topeka told her wisely. "We will have to look for them."

The warriors had made camp as soon as they arrived and were relaxing in the shade. Resting while the women work to fill their stomachs, thought Olive contemptuously. They could at least look for more bushes.

But that, too, was woman's work, and as soon as the bush was stripped of berries, the pickers began wandering off to seek more *oth-to-toa*.

The slopes of the mountain were broken into gulleys and steep rocky ascents, and the vegetation had turned to the browns and yellows of autumn. Before long the snow would come to these elevations. In the thin sunlight of late afternoon it was growing chilly, and Olive wished she had one of the woven rabbit hair capes of the wealthier Mohaves.

She was suddenly aware that she was all alone on the mountain. There had been many searchers in the beginning, but they must have scattered in other directions. She climbed one of the small rises, but although she looked frantically every way, she could see no one. Worst of all, she was turned around. Every gully and slope, every rock and drying bush looked like every other. Where was the camp? Which way had she come? The only thing she knew for sure was that it was somewhere below. She must not climb higher.

She forgot the many times she and Mary Ann had looked at these mountains and discussed the escape that lay on the other side. Even if Mary Ann had been with her, the mountains were too threatening. A body could wander for days, probably in circles, and never find her way out.

Trying to put down her panic, she began the descent. As she walked, she called aloud, first for Topeka, then for anyone who might hear. In her anxiety she forgot to look for *oth-to-toa* bushes. All she wanted was to find someone from the village. Night would come soon, and who knew what wild animals might stalk these mountains after dark.

When finally there was an answer to her call, her heart was thumping so hard she could not answer. She could only stand still and wait. A moment later, a Mohave woman named Katama appeared from behind a ledge of rock.

"Did you find any *oth-to-toa?*" called Katama. She did not seem to notice Olive's frightened face.

Olive shook her head.

"Where there is one, there will be more," said Katama, repeating what Topeka had said.

"Can I stay with you?" begged Olive. "I was lost."

Katama nodded and resumed walking. Olive followed meekly. If she had been asked, she would have said the camp was in the opposite direction. But Indians, she was sure, never got lost.

Suddenly, Katama stopped and held up her hand. Before them was a spur of rock, and from behind it came the unmistakable sounds of someone giggling. The sound was strange in Olive's ears. No one had giggled or laughed in the Mohave village for many weeks. Katama went on, and her face was very stern.

Olive hurried to keep up. When they rounded the spur of rock, they stopped. Sitting on the ground, with their backs propped against the cliff, were the three Cochapa slaves. Beside them were their *chiechucks*. After the first bush had been picked clean, every basket had been a third full of berries. Now they were empty.

"Stupid slaves," said Katama coldly. "What have you done?"

They cowered against the rock, too frightened to speak.

"Your stomachs were empty. Now you have overloaded them with seedy berries. Soon you will be sick," Katama told them. "Get up and walk while you can. We must find the camp."

Without a word the girls rose, took up their empty *chiechucks*, and fell in behind. Olive wondered again about the route they were taking.

131

Surely they must pass something that looked familiar—a rock, a thicket—but everything was strange.

By now it was growing dusk, and perhaps that was why. Things looked different in bright sunlight.

When it grew too dark to see, Katama halted.

"We will stop here," she announced. "It is not good to travel strange trails in the night."

Why, she's lost, thought Olive in surprise. I didn't know Indians ever got lost.

For some time the Cochapa slaves had been making strange sounds as they followed along behind. Now they threw themselves on the ground and moaned in agony. Katama looked at them in disgust.

"They did it to themselves," she said. Then to Olive, "Profit by their mistake. Eat only a handful of the berries. They are mostly seeds, and seeds should be ground in a *metate*. Your stomach, too, is empty."

Olive hardly slept that night. Perhaps it was the cold or the moaning of the three slaves, but whenever she shut her eyes, a hundred terrifying thoughts raced through her mind. If Katama was lost, how would they find the camp? And if she didn't return, but died here on the mountain, what would happen to Mary Ann? She remembered Nowerka's agony on the rude cross. Horrible as it had been, it was over in a few hours. It might take days before she herself died of cold or starvation.

At dawn Katama got up and kicked the slaves awake. By now they had stopped moaning, but Olive had never seen anyone who looked so sick.

"Now we will find the camp," Katama said stoutly.

Olive reached for her *chiechuck*. Every bone ached, and the goose pimples stood up on her skin like welts. Are we just to go walking around and around, she asked herself. Why don't we sit quietly instead and wait for death?

But Katama surprised her. This time she struck a straight course, and within an hour they reached the camp. Only the men were there. All the women were gone.

"Did they find berries?" demanded Katama.

"Yes," answered one of the warriors. Many bushes, well loaded with *oth-to-toa*. He gave directions, and Katama, ordering the slaves to follow, set off at once.

The bushes were not far away, not nearly so far as Olive had walked yesterday, but after her restless night, it required all her reserve strength to go on. She felt sorry for the three Cochapas who had not slept at all.

By late afternoon, all the *chiechucks* were filled to the brim, but the slaves were unable to walk without help. When Katama told the others what had happened, there were some who advised leav-

133

ing them where they were. Anyone who would overload a stomach already shrunken with starvation deserved nothing better. In the end, however, they were helped back to camp, where one of the older Mohave women prepared a brew of special leaves for them to drink. Outside of the incantations and dancing of the shamen, the leaves were the only medicine Olive had ever seen used in the village.

In this case, the leaves did no good. The slaves grew steadily worse. Like everyone in the village, they were half-starved, and the amount of seedy berries they had eaten were too much for their weakened digestive systems. By morning all three were dead.

There were no cries of mourning. Instead, the women began to gather wood. When they had collected enough for a huge fire, the warriors threw the bodies of the dead Cochapa slaves into it.

Olive watched in horror. If she had died, that's what would have happened to her. There was no one to say a prayer or a good word for the deceased. Even Topeka, whom she had thought so kind and sympathetic, seemed to take this cremation as a matter of course. Savages—that's what they were—unfeeling savages!

She sat down as far away as she could from the fire, with her back against a stone and her aching legs thrust out before her. She had never felt so tired. She closed her eyes, and within a minute the crackling sounds of burning wood and the hum of Mohave voices were gone. She was fast asleep.

The next thing she knew, Topeka was shaking her.

"We are going now. Back to the village. Get up."

Olive mumbled protestingly.

"You want to see Mary, don't you?" asked Topeka slyly.

Mary! Mary Ann! Olive stumbled to her feet. They were going home. The *oth-to-toa* was gathered. She could give her sister some of the berries that tasted like oranges. Not too many. Not as many as the slaves had eaten. The memory of the slaves came rushing back, and she darted a quick glance toward the place where the fire had been. It had burned down, and someone had thrown dirt over the ashes and what remained.

"We will travel some of the way tonight since we have rested during the day," Topeka told her. "Pick up your *chiechuck*. We are ready to start."

As she lifted her carrying basket, Olive noticed that three of the warriors now had *chiechucks* fastened on their backs. They must have been those of the dead slaves. The berries would not be wasted.

She remembered little of the trip home. It was all downhill, which helped some, but everyone was tired. There was no talking. They plodded along, each following the one who walked ahead. There was a full moon, so even after the sun had set, it wasn't completely dark, and they stopped but once to drink from a mountain spring. When the moon set, and there were only stars for light, the party halted. But at dawn, they started out again.

In the beginning, Olive's legs had been stiff, but soon they limbered up. After a few hours they grew tired, then because she could not rest, they grew numb. It took effort to make them move at all. She grew light-headed too, and sounds seemed to come from a great way distant. Still she made herself go on. One foot, another foot. It was the way the Mohaves walked, she thought, and giggled senselessly. I'm keeping up with the Mohaves. Perhaps I am a Mohave.

Late on the second day they reached the village. Many who had stayed at home were out to greet them. Espaniol was there, and his dark eyes rested with approval on the baskets filled with *oth-to-toa*.

Topeka stopped to speak with her father, but Olive plodded stiffly on. Neither Mary Ann nor Vimaka had been among those waiting to receive the returning berry pickers.

There were no sounds from the chief's house as she passed through the outer gate. Perhaps Mary Ann was sleeping. Or perhaps—no, she wouldn't let herself think of that. She pushed open the door of laced arrow wood and stood blinking on the threshold.

The single room was dark, as always, but fire glowed in the regular place. Lying on the ground before it was her sister, and Olive did not need a second glance to see that Mary Ann was worse.

Chapter 12

OLIVE FELL TO HER KNEES BESIDE HER SISter, the *chiechuck* bouncing against her shoulders.

"Mary Ann, I'm home. Oh, Mary Ann, how are you?"

"Hungry," said Mary Ann faintly. "Olive, you couldn't get me some bread and milk, could you?"

"No, but I've brought some berries that taste like oranges. You'd like some of them, wouldn't you?"

She felt hands fumbling at her back, and Vimaka took the carrying basket from her.

138

"Fine *oth-to-toa*," she pronounced. "I will mash some in water for the small one. She can drink the juice."

"And perhaps I can find a blackbird's nest," suggested Olive frantically. "You'd like an egg, wouldn't you, Mary Ann?"

"Yes," agreed Mary Ann indifferently. "Olive, I'm going to die."

"Don't talk that way, Mary Ann," she begged, taking the small hand in her own. It was like holding a frail sack of bones.

Vimaka came soon, bearing a gourd filled with liquid, which she held to Mary Ann's lips.

"*Oth-to-toa* juice," she said. "There are no seeds. Seeds would be bad for the small one."

Mary Ann swallowed a few mouthfuls but could not finish because of her coughing. The spell lasted a long time and seemed to tire her, for when it was over, she fell asleep.

"You rest now," Vimaka told Olive, and she tugged loose a corner of the blanket that covered Mary Ann so it would also cover her sister.

Olive nodded. Yes, she would rest, for she had never felt so tired in her life. But she did not let go of the small bony hand.

For four days she stayed as close as she could to Mary Ann's side. Vimaka made no demands on her during that time, but on occasion Olive left voluntarily in search of food. Perhaps there was a root nearby that had been overlooked. And even though it was not the season, she might be lucky and find a bird's nest with eggs. Her frantic searches resulted in nothing, but it made her feel better to try. She was light-headed herself from hunger, and the burning in her stomach never stopped.

When the chief's household had food, Vimaka always made sure to give some to the slaves, but there were times when they too went hungry, for the storage bags for mesquite beans and seeds hung empty from the roof. The cries of mourning for those newly dead of starvation went on day and night, and the tang of smoke from the funeral pyres was constantly in the air.

On the fifth morning after Olive's return from the mountains, Vimaka brought Mary Ann her usual gourd of *oth-to-toa* juice, and as she drank it, the woman leaned close and peered into the girl's face. Immediately she began to cry and moan, beating her bare chest with her hands.

"Don't cry," said Mary Ann. "I am going to God. I'll see my Ma and Pa again, and all my brothers and sisters. There's nothing to cry about."

"Don't say that, Mary Ann." Olive's voice was harsher than she intended it to be. Vimaka's actions had frightened her.

"Let's sing," suggested Mary Ann. "What shall we sing, Olive?"

"You must save your strength," objected Olive anxiously.

Instead, Mary Ann began one of the hymns they had performed so many times for the Mohaves. Surprisingly, her voice seemed stronger today.

> "The day is past and gone,
>   The evening shades appear."

Vimaka stopped crying and beating her breast, and after a moment Olive did her best to join in. When they finished the song, Mary Ann began a second, and this time Olive was able to keep her voice steady. If Mary Ann felt like singing, surely she must be better.

She was aware that Espaniol's little house was beginning to fill with people, and she was not surprised. The Indians always gathered to listen when they were singing. And they were always quiet, as now. Finally Mary Ann stopped.

"I can't sing anymore," she said. "But don't cry, Olive. I don't want you to cry."

"Mary Ann," cried Olive wildly. "Stop!"

But it was too late. Mary Ann had closed her eyes. Vimaka was keening again, as well as some of the Indian women who had crowded around. Olive felt gentle hands on her shoulders, and heard Topeka's voice in her ear.

"Come away," said Topeka. "And rejoice that her spirit did not go down a rat hole."

For a time Olive was too numb with shock to think. Then gradually she became aware that plans were underway to dispose of Mary Ann's body in the Mohave manner by fire. The numbness was suddenly gone, as though someone had thrown icy water in her face.

"They can't do that. I won't let them," she told Vimaka and Topeka loudly. "It's not our way. Mary Ann must be buried in the ground so she can rise again on Judgment Day."

Topeka shook her head doubtfully, but Vimaka patted Olive's shoulder reassuringly.

"I will speak with the chief," she promised. "I am not without influence with that one."

She was gone a long time, but when she returned she was nodding with satisfaction.

"The chief thinks it is a great foolishness, but he says you may do as you please," she announced. "He will even give a blanket to wrap the small one in, and she shall wear the beads she earned by singing. Two men are even now digging a great hole by the riverbank near the place where you planted your garden."

"You are good," said Olive, and her eyes swam with tears. She wished again there was a Mohave word for thank you, but she was sure Vimaka understood.

All the Mohaves attended the ceremony of laying Mary Ann to rest beside the river. Some came to scoff at this queer custom of the *hiccos*, but others came to mourn. Mary Ann had made many friends, Olive thought in surprise, as she looked at the solemn faces, some stained with tears.

It wasn't a proper funeral, she knew, for there was no one to say the service. But she bowed her head and repeated the Lord's Prayer as two Mohaves lowered the small blanket-wrapped form into the pit they had made with the implements used for digging holes to bake maguey bulbs. Olive didn't even have a bunch of flowers to lay upon the mound, she thought sadly. She would have liked to plant a wild rose bush, for Mary Ann had always loved the pink fragrant blossoms, but remembering what had happened to their corn crop, she decided against it. Someone might pull the roots from the ground for spite. There were many in the tribe, like Cearekae, who had little use for whites.

Now that Mary Ann was gone, Olive had nothing to live for. She spent most of her time crouched in the darkest corner of the chief's house and hardly answered when someone spoke to her. She knew she was going to die, just as Mary Ann had done, and she didn't care. All around her, Indians were dying every day. She only wished death could come soon so the pains in her stomach would go away. Without the need to find food for her sister, she saw no need to go outside the door. Before long she was too weak to walk more than a few steps.

Vimaka watched her with anxious eyes, and one day when they were alone, she brought Olive a little gruel made of pounded corn and water.

"Tell no one," she warned. "Drink it quickly, so there will be no traces in the bowl."

There was no need to tell her that. Olive gulped it down hungrily. But when she asked for more, Vimaka shook her head.

"Tomorrow," she promised. "Now you will have the juice of the *oth-to-toa*. Remember, tell no one."

For three days Olive received a bowl of pounded corn when Vimaka was sure they would not be disturbed, and it gave her a little strength. Even more important was the realization that the chief's wife had dipped into her scanty store of seed corn for the next harvest. It didn't matter that Vimaka was a savage. She was kind. And she must want me to live, Olive told herself, or she wouldn't have done that. It was comforting to know that at least one person was concerned with her welfare. For Vimaka's sake, she got up and began staggering around, a little more each day.

How anyone managed to survive that winter, Olive never knew. The hunters went out and brought back occasional game. A party crossed the mountains and returned with a few supplies from the friendly Yumas. Perhaps someone had a hidden hoard of edible seeds and roots that was produced and divided. Olive never asked the source of the food in her bowl. She only ate what Vimaka gave her once a day without even noticing that now Vimaka was dividing the portions equally.

All traces of fat had disappeared from Mohave bodies, and bones protruded into flesh. There was always a dizziness in Olive's head and a great aching void in her stomach. One day was like the next, and they all seemed to run together in a jumble. She thought often of Mary Ann and hoped Ma understood that Olive had done the best she could for her little sister. At least Mary Ann wasn't hungry anymore. Maybe there was bread and milk in heaven.

One morning she awoke to find that she was alone. Chief Espaniol, Vimaka, and Topeka had gone, leaving her asleep. They had left the door ajar, and through it a streamer of sunshine lay across the dirt floor. Olive lay there for a moment, wondering what was different about this day. But as soon as she had struggled to her feet and looked out the door, she knew. Winter had slipped away with the night!

There was little warmth in the sunshine, but it was welcome anyway. Above the acrid tang of smoking fires, there was another smell, a smell of growing things within the earth. Soon there would be sprigs and leaves to betray the life-giving roots below. There was the smell of the river, too, and the sound of its voice as it pushed against the bank. Before many days it would cover the land

145

that would provide gardens for the Mohaves. It would even cover Mary Ann's grave, but the thought was not upsetting. The river was friendly and life-giving. It was not all destructive like fire.

Topeka rounded the corner of the fenced enclosure, and as she stood, a *chiechuck* bobbing on her back, her face wore a happpy smile.

"Look," she said, turning so that Olive could see into the basket. "The winter wheat is ripening, and I found some young roots. Today we will have something good to put in our stomachs."

Chapter 13

THE YEAR THAT FOLLOWED THE FAMINE was one of feasting. Not only were the garden patches heavy with produce, but the bushes on the hillside were loaded with wild berries and nuts. Vimaka's storage bags bulged once again with mesquite beans and edible seeds, and even tribesmen who usually had no luck trapping fish from the muddy Colorado brought back record catches.

Olive was pounding mesquite one day in the sunny doorway of Espaniol's house when she saw four strangers ride into the village. They were Yumas. She could tell because one wore a white man's ragged shirt, and their feet were without moccasins. The Mohaves said the Yumas had feet as hard as bear hide and needed no protection. After the first glance, she thought no more about it.

The Yumas and Mohaves were constant visitors in each others' villages. There was much trading between the tribes. The Yumas liked the produce raised in Mohave gardens, their rabbit hair blankets and skillfully made pottery. In exchange, they bartered articles obtained from the whites who maintained a fort somewhere in their territory, bits of the prized red flannel, beads and even scraps of iron that could be made into spear- or arrowheads.

A crowd had gathered around the Yuma horses, women and children as well as men, and Olive could hear their voices clamoring for news. She could not hear the visitors' responses, but they must have been displeasing to the Mohaves, for they were received with growls and protests.

Maybe another war, she thought listlessly. And if a warrior is killed in battle, a slave will have to be sacrificed. The thought that she herself was the only remaining slave in the village did not bring the fear that it had in the Cochapa raid. She had been lonely since Mary Ann's death. Dying might not be so bad—so long as it was quick.

The Yuma visitors and some of the Mohave

148

braves began moving in her direction, and she was not surprised. They were probably going to have a council, and naturally, it would be in the house of the chief. But she was surprised to see Topeka rush ahead of the group and run swiftly toward her. She had not even noticed Topeka in the crowd.

"Quick," cried Topeka, when she reached her side. She pulled Olive to her feet, spilling the half-pounded mesquite recklessly on the ground. "You must not be here when they come. I will hide you in Adpadorama's house."

"But why?" Olive let herself be pulled along, after a rueful glance at the spilled mesquite. Vimaka wouldn't like that one bit.

"Who are they? What do they want?" she demanded, when Topeka had rushed her through the village to the farthest house and pushed her inside.

"The leader is Francisco. A Yuma," added Topeka unnecessarily. "He is trying to get you away from us. He says he will give you to the whites, but we know that is a lie. The Yumas want you for themselves. Now stay here. Don't open the door. I'll return when it's safe."

Olive's knees gave way, and she sank to the dirt floor.

"Wait," she called weakly. "Don't go, Topeka."

But Topeka had already closed the door and was hurrying away.

Olive sat in the stuffy darkness of Adpadorama's house, trying to realize what had happened. There were no windows, and only a little light came from the smoke hole in the roof. She stared down at her legs, tanned by the sun so they were just a shade or two lighter than the Mohaves'. She looked at the moccasins Vimaka had made for her, unadorned by trimming, but sturdy enough to withstand the rough trails to the berry fields. The shredded bark petticoat, which reached just above her knees, was Vimaka's handiwork too, and the horrible blue lines of tattooing on her chin—she reached up and covered them with her hand—marked her as Mohave. How had Francisco, or anyone else, known she was white?

Then she realized that there was always talk. The Yumas had been coming here for years, long before she and Mary Ann had been taken captive. They would have heard of the purchase of two white slaves. But why, at this late date—Olive had lost track of time—were they coming for her now? It was a Yuma brave who had found and brought Nowerka back after her escape. If what the man said was true and he was here to return her to her own people, why was he doing it?

She knew there were whites, even a fort with soldiers, in Yuma territory. Perhaps word of a captive white girl had finally reached their ears, and they had sent Francisco to bring her back. At the thought, she felt a great stirring of hope. It was

150

almost too much to expect. No one could be as secretive as an Indian unless—unless his tongue was loosened· by *tulibai*. Could that have happened?

Or was it, as Topeka said, that the Yumas themselves had decided they wanted her as a slave? She didn't think that was likely. It would mean risking the long-standing friendship between the two tribes. And besides, living as they did in the proximity of the whites, it would be dangerous. No, the man must be telling the truth.

She sat still, straining her ears for sounds from the outside, but there were none. Adpadorama's house was at one end of the village. Espaniol's was at the other, and all the Mohaves were gathered there. She got up and opened the arrowweed door a crack, but the distance was too great to hear anything. She would have liked to venture out, to creep closer, but Topeka had told her to remain here, and she was afraid to disobey.

All afternoon and far into the night, she stayed in the stuffy house. Late in the day, hunger impelled her to take a handful of *attileka* nuts from a bag hanging from the roof, but she was afraid to take enough to fill her stomach. Mesepa, Adpadorama's wife, lacked Vimaka's foresight, and there were only a few storage bags ready for the winter months.

When it was very late, Olive heard sounds within the enclosure, and when the door was

151

pushed open, she recognized the whining voice of Mesepa coming from the darkness.

"Get her out of my house. You had no right to bring the *hicco* here without my permission."

"Yours was the farthest house in the village. I thought she would be safest here." This was Topeka, calm as always, and a little haughty as befitting the daughter of a chief. "She did no harm."

"She should be killed." Mesepa's voice grew shrill. "Many agree. You heard them yourself. She has brought trouble on the village and ill will between the Mohaves and the Yumas. No slave is worth that."

"Come, Olive," said Topeka, ignoring the woman. "Francisco has gone back across the river. It is safe to come home now."

Olive followed her meekly into the starry night. After the darkness of the house, it seemed very light outside. They passed many groups of Mohaves, returning to their own homes after the council. Olive could tell by their angry glares that most of them agreed with Mesepa. Whatever had taken place in the council had not added to her popularity.

Even Espaniol, when they returned to the house, was not himself. His dark eyes rested on Olive resentfully, and he did not speak to her.

Vimaka had been stirring something in a pot, and her brown face glowed in the light of the fire.

"Clay and ashes," she told Topeka. "It will be ready in the morning."

Topeka nodded without speaking, then motioned Olive to lie down on her sleeping mat. It was clear that whatever had transpired in the council was not going to be discussed that night. Nor was there to be an evening meal.

Sleep was slow in coming. Olive lay awake long after the snoring of Espaniol and Vimaka and the rhythmic breathing of Topeka filled the little house. What was going to happen to her? The Mohaves were angry. Even those who had once seemed friendly had turned away on the short walk through the village. Perhaps, as Mesepa had suggested, they would kill her, or at the very least they would sell her to another tribe.

She had no confidence in Francisco and the three Yumas who accompanied him. What could four men do against a whole tribe? And even if they were successful in getting her away from the Mohaves, there was no guarantee that they would return her to her own people.

She didn't know when she dropped off, but she couldn't have slept long. Her bones were still tired and her eyes heavy when Vimaka shook her awake.

"Get up," she ordered. "We must make you ready before Francisco crosses the river."

The purpose of the pot filled with clay and ashes soon became clear. Vimaka began smearing the mixture over Olive's body, her arms and legs, her back and chest and face. They soon dried to a grayish film, so the skin color beneath was invisible.

"She does not look like a *hicco* now," said Topeka approvingly. She had been watching the proceedings intently, occasionally pointing out a spot her mother had missed. "But she does not look like an Indian either," she added.

"You will tell Francisco that you are of a different race, one that is far from here," ordered Vimaka. "Not American. Tell him you are not American."

Olive, looking down at the gray coating, silently agreed that she looked like no race she had ever seen. She was more like a ghost.

Before long the members of the Mohave council began crowding through the doorway. Vimaka and Topeka had to leave to join the lesser tribesmen, but they hovered as closely as they dared outside the walls.

"Do not speak American," ordered Topeka, before she left. "Francisco may know some words of their language. Speak only sounds that mean nothing."

Eventually, Francisco and the other three Yumas were ushered inside the house. Only Francisco wore a white man's shirt, so obviously he was the most distinguished of the group. Their feet were bare, with widespread toes, and their long, braided

154

hair was coated with some substance Olive could not identify. All of them wore earrings made of shell and bone, and two had rings through their noses.

But the thing that caught and held her eye was a white paper clutched in Francisco's hand. It had been so many years since she had seen paper of any kind that it took a moment to identify it.

"A letter," she gasped in English. "You have a letter."

The Mohaves scowled and murmured fiercely, but Francisco beamed and flourished the paper.

"I bring talking paper from the head man of the fort," he announced proudly, waving the envelope beneath Espaniol's nose. "It says words to the chief of the Mohave."

"I cannot tell what the words say," Espaniol told him scornfully. "They are probably lies."

"I can read them," said Olive in a small voice, and again the council muttered angrily.

"Read. Read," invited Francisco, thrusting the paper in her hand.

Without looking at the angry faces all around her, Olive took the envelope. How smooth the paper was! She had forgotten how smooth. Although it was soiled from handling, she thought how white it must have been at one time.

On the outside of the envelope a flourishing hand had written, "Francisco, a Yuma Indian, going to the Mohave." She stared at the swirling lines, and her eyes filled with tears. A white man had written those words—a member of her own race.

Slowly, carefully, she broke the seal and took out the single sheet within. It read:

Francisco, Yuma Indian, bearer of this, goes to the Mohave Nation to obtain a white woman there, named Olivia. It is desirable that she should come to this post or send her reasons why she does not wish to come.

Martin Burke

Lieut. Col., Commanding

Headquarters, Fort Yuma, Cal.,

27th January, 1856

Olive read the letter several times. Her own people knew where she was! They hadn't forgotten her! Her captivity by the Indians was at an end, and it was almost more than she could take in.

Neither the Mohaves nor Francisco had been quiet while she was studying the letter. Dimly, she could hear their arguing voices. The Mohaves were insisting that Olive was not the white woman he sought. Look at her, they cried. Did she look white? Had he ever seen a white with skin that color? And Francisco was answering that yes, she was white. What they had done to her skin was a trick. He had seen her before on other visits to the Mohaves. She was white, like the men at the

156

fort, and unless she was returned, soldiers would come with guns and kill all the Mohaves.

"What does it say?" demanded Espaniol, roughly shaking Olive's shoulder. "What does the talking paper say?"

With dry lips and a choking voice, she read the first sentence. When she glanced up, black angry eyes stared back at her suspiciously, and she knew that the words of the colonel were too mild. She must make them stronger. The Mohaves would think of a hundred reasons why she did not want to accompany Francisco and make her say them.

"Unless she is returned at once," she improvised, staring at the paper blankly and trying to make her voice as threatening as she could, "the Americans will send a large army and destroy any Mohave they can find. And if Francisco does not turn her over to us, we will kill all the Yumas, too."

When she finished speaking, there was a moment of silence, then everyone began talking at once. Some advised that Olive be killed and Francisco report that she was already dead. Others claimed their own braves could outfight any American army. A few said to let her go; she was not worth any trouble.

"Outside!" shouted Espaniol above the turmoil. "The slave and the Yumas go outside. It is a matter for the council to decide."

Rough hands began pushing her from the room, but in the moment before Topeka rushed up to claim her, Olive had a moment to speak with Francisco.

"Thank you," she said in English. "Thank you for risking your life for me."

"I will be paid," he told her proudly. "I am to have a horse."

"But how did the Americans know I was here?" She hated to let him go and strained against Topeka's efforts to get her away.

"Your older brother has friends," said Francisco, shrugging. "They have been working."

"My brother? Lorenzo? But he was killed by the Apaches."

"Maybe not," said Francisco cheerfully. "Today he lives."

Topeka finally won the tug of war and drew her away. Olive hardly noticed. Lorenzo alive! But she had seen him herself, lying on the ground, the back of his head covered with blood. He had not resisted, not even when they pulled the shoes from his feet. But what reason would Francisco have for lying? She wondered if there were any other survivors. Ma? Pa? Lucy? One of the younger children?

"I told you not to talk American," said Topeka crossly. "You may have spoiled everything."

Olive didn't bother to answer. She sat on the ground, some distance from the Mohaves who were crowded close around the chief's house, trying to catch some snatches of the discussion going on inside. For the first time since that terrible night—was it five years ago?—Olive felt alive, as though she was at last making her way out of a long nightmare.

Several hours later the door opened, and the Yumas were summoned back to the council. This time Olive was not invited in. She, who had the most at stake, must stay outside while others decided her fate.

From time to time Topeka spoke to her, but what she said Olive did not know. She heard herself answering, but whether her words replied to the questions did not matter. All that was important was the decision being made inside the house.

It was after dusk when the doors finally opened and the council members came pouring out. It took no explanations to tell her what the decision had been, for the Mohaves were scowling while the Yumas were smiling widely.

"We leave at sunup," Francisco told Olive proudly.

And Espaniol added in a threatening tone, "Topeka will go also. Francisco has promised that the *hiccos* will give me a horse. She will bring it back."

Chapter 14

ALTHOUGH TOPEKA WAS SORRY TO LOSE OLIVE, of whom she had grown fond, she had a reason for being glad of the council's decision. Cearekae had been appointed in charge of the company of braves who would accompany the white slave to the soldiers' fort. It was a great honor and had come about because of his bravery in the battle against the Cochapas. It was evident that his standing in the tribe had risen, and that his worth was being recognized.

Moreover, since she herself would be in the

same party, there might be an opportunity for them to have a little time together. Cearekae was very shy. He recognized the great gulf that separated a chief's daughter from one of the younger braves. So far, he had made no opportunity to speak to her and had given no evidence that he regarded her as being different from any other Mohave girl. Topeka was determined to put an end to that.

Long before sunrise, she rolled up her sleeping mat and began dressing herself for the trail. She chose her sturdiest moccasins and carefully shook her fiber bark skirt free from burrs and dust. She filled a little bag with *attileka* nuts and tied it about her waist, then poured mashed mesquite seeds into a gourd to take along. She hesitated a long time over the four strings of blue and white beads, one more strand than any other Mohave maiden owned, but in the end she left them where they were. They could catch on snags or branches. She smoothed all tangles from her long black hair, cut square above her eyebrows and hanging loose to her hips, and pronounced herself ready for the journey.

Through the dim light coming from the open doorway, she could see that Olive was also prepared. She had hung her single strand of beads, earned from singing for the guests, about her neck and had tied back her hair with the strip of red flannel Espaniol had given her. Except for the bark petticoat and moccasins Vimaka had made for her, they were her only possessions. Topeka felt a little pang of regret as her eyes fell on those worn moccasins. It was too bad her mother had not trimmed them with a little fringe or decoration. But that might have made trouble. There were those in the tribe who felt that any moccasins at all were more than a slave deserved.

Vimaka was stirring something in a pot over the small cooking fire. Topeka identified the smell —stewed pumpkin and *serecca* seeds, with a fish head added for flavor and nourishment. She smiled affectionately at her mother. Normally, the family breakfast would not be until midmorning, but Vimaka did not want her daughter and the white slave to walk all day with empty stomachs. She knew that the party would not halt for food until late afternoon.

Espaniol awakened with a snort, stretched, and then got to his feet. Without a glance at anyone he stalked outside, and Topeka knew he was still angry. He had cause for anger, she thought sadly. He had paid the Apaches well for the two white slaves and had treated them kindly. They had lived in his house, shared his food, and he had even been tolerant of their foolish *hicco* customs. Hadn't he allowed Mary to be buried in the ground, instead of being decently burned? He had overridden Kitkilha's protests and ordered their faces to be tattooed as a precaution for their spirits

162

after death. A dozen times he had protected them from tribesmen who felt the white slaves might bring misfortune on the villlage. And how had he been rewarded? One slave had died, and the other was voluntarily returning to her own people.

Vimaka began ladling portions of the stew into two bowls.

"Eat," she said.

Topeka accepted her serving, and Olive stepped forward for hers. As she took it, she said a strange American word that neither of the Mohave women understood.

As they were leaving the house, Vimaka began to cry. "I will miss you," she told Olive. "You have been like another daughter in this house."

Olive put her arms around the plump figure, and Topeka could see that she was crying, too.

"I shall miss you also, Vimaka," Olive said. "And I can never forget all that you have done for me. You saved my life when I was starving. You got permission to bury my sister in the Christian manner. I will never be able to—" Here she ended with that strange American word.

"It is time to go," Topeka reminded them. "The sun is nearly up."

They went outside, and it seemed the whole of the village was there to see the departure. Most of the faces were angry, and several Mohaves spat disdainfully as they passed. Only a few seemed sorry to see the white slave go.

163

Adpadorama stalked up to them and with a ruthless hand jerked the beads from Olive's neck, breaking the sinew thread that held them. Then he snatched the red flannel from her hair.

"These belong to the Mohave," he said insolently.

Topeka was indignant at his actions. Olive had earned those small tokens, and they should have been hers to take away. But she dared not say so to Adpadorama, who was second in tribal command and who, some people said, would be Espaniol's successor when he had gone with the Ghost Chief. But because she could not speak her feelings on this matter, she tried to make it up to Olive in another way.

"There would be a moment to visit the spot where Mary lies under the earth, if you would like to go," she suggested.

Olive nodded, her eyes suddenly full of tears again, and Topeka, ignoring the warriors waiting to accompany them, led the way to the riverbank.

It would have been hard for Topeka to find the place, since the river's last flooding had leveled the mound. But Olive seemed to know. She closed her eyes, her lips moved silently, then she turned away.

"You don't think they might dig up Mary Ann's body and burn it?" she asked fearfully. "Your father is angry with me, so I don't think he will protect the grave anymore."

164

Topeka knew that such a thing was quite possible, but there was no need to make Olive unhappy. Even though she was an ungrateful girl and had deliberately disobeyed orders, which might have meant she could stay with the Mohaves, she had been a good slave and there was no need to punish her now.

"I don't think they could find it," she replied.

Cearekae and three other young warriors, who had been named to accompany the girls and the Yumas, were waiting. Espaniol's orders were to make sure the slave was turned over to the whites and not kept by the Yumas themselves. Although the tribes were friends, even friends would bear watching. A white slave was a valuable possession.

They swam the river to join Francisco's men on the opposite shore, and Topeka was glad she had insisted that Olive and Mary learn how to swim. She had been astonished to find that they didn't know how, and that only white boys swam in rivers. Mary had never been able to master more than a few strokes, but Olive had learned rapidly. A good thing too, Topeka told herself. They must swim more than one stream before they reached the country of the Yumas.

The trail was rough and difficult, as were all trails.

"I'm glad we only have to travel two days," said Olive when they stopped for a brief rest after several hours.

"Two suns?" Topeka looked at her in surprise. "It is two suns to the top of the mountains where the Mohaves and the Yumas keep a camp for runners. That way we can relay news between the tribes. We must travel nine or ten suns before we reach the place where the *hiccos* have their soldier fort."

"Oh," said Olive in a surprised tone. Her face suddenly took on a strange look. "I thought it was closer than that. The tribes visit each other so often."

"The Mohaves are great walkers," Topeka reminded her proudly. "And so are the Yumas. The trail is not easy. When you first came here, you would not have been able to make it. But now you will not slow us up too much."

Olive had grown strong in the years she had spent with the Mohaves. This would not be like the trip they had made from the Apache camp when she was barely able to put one foot before the other. She could scale fallen logs, climb rocks, and swim rivers, and she was not always crying that she must stop and rest. By now Olive knew which berries to pick and which to leave alone, how to find hidden bulbs and roots even when there were no telltale shoots to betray their presence underground. She could carry great loads of firewood and water and was learning to tan hides and even make creditable pottery.

Why, Topeka asked herself, when she had showed such promise, did Olive want to return to the thieving whites, the *hiccos*? Surely she could find some fine young Mohave for a husband. But not Cearekae. Cearekae was Topeka's, and every day she grew more certain of it.

That night as they sat around their fire, warming their feet against the chill of the mountain air, she managed to place her blanket next to Cearekae's. They did not look at each other, but she was very aware of his nearness, and she knew he was aware of her.

"This is a hard trail for a woman," he said once, staring intently at a smoldering log.

"I have traveled harder," she told him, trying to keep her voice matter of fact and without show of boastfulness.

"I have heard," said Cearekae. "The daughter of our chief is very strong."

On the second night they reached the permanent camp on the mountaintop, and the Yuma runner stationed there left immediately to tell his people that Francisco had been successful in his mission. The white slave was on her way.

It was there that Cearekae performed an act that made Topeka grow warm with happiness. He cut some leafy boughs to make her bed more comfortable.

"The ground is rocky," he observed, staring

hard at a cloud on the horizon. "Perhaps the leaves will help the daughter of the chief to sleep more restfully."

On the third night, as they sat about the fire, he became bold indeed.

"Many wonder why the daughter of the chief has not taken a husband," he said.

"Because I will not marry an old man," Topeka told him daringly. "They are fat, and their muscles are soft. Sometimes their breath has a bad smell, and there are lice in their hair."

She wondered if she had gone too far when he got up hastily and changed his place at the fire. But the next morning she saw that he had coated his hair with clay. If there were lice, they would wash out with the clay in a few days' time.

The weather grew hotter as they approached the place where the *hiccos* had built their fort. It was not land that Topeka would have liked to call her own. There were high mountains with great stretches of desert behind on which only aloe and cactus grew. The Colorado, life blood of the Mohave, flowed here too, but in Yuma country it did not seem like the same river, for it was yellow and sluggish, and like the land itself, it looked steamy.

Francisco pointed out the army post on the top of an adjacent bluff across the river. The buildings were the color of sand, square and unfriendly, with a piece of colored cloth hanging limply from the top of a tall tree from which all limbs had been stripped. Topeka stared at it in distaste. Was this what Olive preferred to the noisy, friendly Mohave village beside a cool, gurgling river? She couldn't believe it.

As they stood there on the bank, a wooden contrivance of some kind pushed off from the opposite shore and started toward them. It was not a canoe, but more like a raft, and two men kept it on course by dipping poles into the water.

"It is called a ferry," said Francisco proudly. "It will cross the river and take us to the other side."

The Mohaves looked at one another in consternation. They had no wish to trust their lives to such a thing.

"*Hiccos!*" said Cearekae suddenly. "Look at them!"

A multitude of whites had begun pouring from the opened gates of the wall that surrounded the buildings. Some were soldiers in uniform. Some were men in the sort of clothes Americans generally wore. A few wore long flowing skirts that swept the ground.

At the sight of them, Olive gave a little cry and ran behind a bush.

"What is the matter with her?" demanded Cearekae, frowning. "Why does she hide herself?"

Topeka didn't know, so she followed Olive to inquire.

"Oh, the shame," cried Olive. Her face was

169

buried in her hands, making it hard to understand her. "I cannot let them see me like this. They're my own people."

"Have you changed your mind?" asked Topeka kindly. "Do you no longer want to go to the white man's fort? It is not too late to change your mind."

"I want to go. But not dressed like this. Topeka, let me have your blanket to wrap around me."

But this Topeka refused to do. Blankets were hard to come by and expensive. She would never be able to explain the loss of a blanket to her father. Besides, the whole thing was silly. Olive looked very well. It was too bad Adpadorama had taken her string of beads, but the bark petticoat had held up surprisingly well, considering the difficulties of the trail.

"Come out," she ordered. "The *hiccos* are nearly here with their strange canoe."

"Tell them to go back and bring me a blanket," insisted Olive stubbornly. "They'll understand that I must be covered up."

Topeka shrugged. If the whites wanted to waste a blanket and a second trip on a foolish girl, it was nothing to her. She left the privacy of the bush and relayed the message to Francisco who could translate to the ferryman. Olive was here. She refused to leave the security of the bush until she had something to cover her body.

170

The ferryman argued a little, but in a moment he began untying the ropes that by now moored his bark to the shore.

"And tell him to bring the horse, too," shouted Cearekae. "We'll give you the girl when we get the horse. We will not cross the river."

Again Francisco translated the demand, and Topeka looked at Cearekae in admiration. How smart he was! She certainly had no desire to cross the river, and she had forgotten about the horse. Now everything was taken care of.

This time Cearekae looked at her directly. For a long moment they gazed into each other's eyes before they turned away.

The opposite bank had become crowded with whites. Topeka had never seen so many in one gathering before. She was glad she didn't have to accompany Olive across the river to claim the horse. She went behind the bush to see how the girl was getting along.

"There are many of your people waiting to greet you," she said.

"I know," agreed Olive. "I can see them through the leaves. That's why I have to be covered. I couldn't meet them naked as a savage."

Topeka understood the word savage, and she was offended. She left abruptly and returned to the Indians waiting on the bank.

There seemed to be some scrambling about when the ferryman delivered his message on the opposite shore. Several people left the group and went inside the walled fort. Presently a man returned, leading a horse. It was black, and Topeka was pleased. Her father would be happy, since there were only brown horses in the tribe.

The animal was led, rather unwillingly, onto the ferry and tied. Then one of the whites in long, flapping skirts came running to thrust a bundle into the ferryman's hands. A moment or two later, they pushed off again.

"A black horse is a fine prize," said Cearekae. Topeka hadn't noticed that he had come to stand beside her.

"My father will be happy," she answered.

"I wish it were mine," said Cearekae. "It would make a fitting bride price."

"You are looking for a bride? With such a horse you could have your choice among the maidens."

"I have but one choice. And I have but one horse," Cearekae admitted. "He is too old to be of value as a bride price. He belonged to my father."

"Perhaps he is not too old to sire a colt if you could find a mare," she suggested.

"That is true," agreed Cearekae seriously. "But the owner of the mare would claim the colt."

"That would depend on many things," she told him. "If this horse is a mare, I could ask my father for the colt. I do not think he would deny me."

"But your father has only stallions," he reminded her.

"This horse may be a mare," Topeka said again. "If the colt were mine, I could give it to the one I chose," she argued. "Then it could be used as a bride price."

"But now you have no colt," Cearekae reminded her sadly. Then he added, "I am a young man. I shall get a new horse. I will steal one from the enemy."

She nodded.

"I am not fat and my muscles are strong," he continued doggedly. "I have cleaned the lice from my hair, and I do not think my breath is offensive."

"Nor do I," she agreed, and they smiled in understanding.

When the ferry again reached the bank where they were standing, the ferryman tossed a cloth bundle ashore.

"There's clothes for the girl," he shouted. "I won't untie the horse till she comes aboard."

Topeka ran forward and snatched up the bundle. It felt curiously light in her grasp. If it was a blanket, it would give small protection against the cold.

Tears ran down Olive's cheeks as she unfolded the bundle. It proved to be a garment made with long, flapping skirts like some of the *hiccos* across the river were wearing. Topeka watched curiously as Olive put it on and awkwardly did up the row of tiny fastenings from the high neck to the waist. It was a dull gray color with a tiny design in black, and it covered her from her chin to the ground, with long sleeves that concealed her wrists.

"A dress," said Olive, sobbing and smoothing the material with rough hands. "I never thought I'd wear one again."

Topeka thought she had never seen a garment quite so ugly, but she didn't say so. Olive's pleasure was too evident.

"I'll say good-bye, Topeka," said Olive, clasping her about the shoulders. "And—" Here again was that strange American word. She walked out of the thicket, and Topeka saw that one hand, in a curious gesture, was tightly covering her chin. It must be some strange greeting custom of the *hiccos*, she told herself.

A great cheer went up from the opposite bank when Olive appeared, and as soon as she stepped onto the ferry, the boatman began untying the black horse. Cearekae stepped forward to take it.

"It's a mare," he told Topeka a moment later, giving the rope into her hands.

"Yes," she agreed happily. "I see. It must be an omen."

Author's Note

In the year 1850, Royce Oatman, his wife and seven children left Independence, Missouri, in the company of fifty people bent on founding a New Zion in New Mexico. Because of quarreling and bickering among themselves, the party divided. Then families began dropping out at various small settlements along the way. At a Pima village, ninety miles from Tucson, the Oatman wagon continued on alone. On March 19, 1851, it was attacked by a band of Tonto Apaches, and the whole family, with the exception of Lorenzo, 15,

175

Olive, 12, and Mary Ann, 7, were killed. Lorenzo was left for dead but later revived and was taken west by another emigrant train. Olive and Mary Ann became captives of the Tontos, but a year later were sold as slaves to the Mohaves. Mary Ann, who presumably was in the early stages of tuberculosis at the time, later died during a period of famine from which many tribal members also succumbed. In 1856, Olive's plight became known to the American forces at Fort Yuma, and she was rescued with the aid of a friendly Yuma Indian named Francisco.

In 1857, Lorenzo Oatman procured the services of the Reverend R. B. Stratton to write their story, which was published in book form that same year by Carlton & Porter. Presumably both Olive and Lorenzo cooperated with the Reverend Mr. Stratton in the preparation of CAPTIVITY OF THE OATMAN GIRLS, BEING AN INTERESTING NARRATIVE OF LIFE AMONG THE APACHE & MOHAVE INDIANS.

Certainly, the bare facts are given, as well as some of the details of Indian life, but the reader must ferret them out from such an overflow of flowery rhetoric that the thread of the narrative is often obscured. The Reverend Mr. Stratton claims, in his preface, to give only facts in "a simple, plain, comprehensive manner," but he also states that for the eleven years previous to this time he has been engaged in public speaking. It shows. The style of orators who once held forth at Fourth of July celebrations and in many early pulpits springs out from every page. Even when he gives a direct quote from one of his characters, I doubt if it is literal. My own grandmother, who was two years younger than Olive when she crossed the plains with her parents, and none of her peers whom I remember from old-time pioneer picnics ever spoke like that. Not that they wouldn't have liked to. And that's probably why they devoured the book. Over 25,000 copies were sold. Amazingly, the first two printings of 11,000 copies were exhausted in a few months in Oregon Territory and California—at a time when the hardworking settlers had scant time to devote to reading of any kind. In a small way, the book probably did as much to turn public sentiment against the Indians as *Uncle Tom's Cabin* did against Negro slavery.

Over a hundred years later, it is possible to look at Olive's experience a little more dispassionately. A study of tribal customs shows that neither tribe was unnecessarily cruel. She worked hard, but so did the Indian women. Olive conceded that, but she remained bitter that the men did not join in the work.

She gives disappointingly few proper names, or perhaps Mr. Stratton thought they were unimportant. Only Toaquin, of all the Tonto Apaches, is singled out. In the Mohave tribe, she mentions

Topeka, Espaniol, Cearekae, and Adpadorama. The wife of Espaniol, who was especially kind to her, remains nameless. I have called her Vimaka, which in the Mohave tongue means Bean Mesquite.

I have no idea whether a romance developed between Topeka and Cearekae, but it could have. Topeka was seventeen at the time Olive was sold by the Apaches, two years older than was usual for a Mohave girl to marry, and she was still living in her father's house. There had to be a reason for that. Since Olive says Topeka was attractive, spritely, and intelligent, I thought it was time she found a husband.

After the publication of the book, Olive launched into personal appearance tours, lecturing on the evils of Indian ways. Most of these performances were under the auspices of churches. She was never able to remove the lines of tattooing from her chin, although several attempts were made to do so.

Later she married, and since she had no children of her own, she took in orphans to rear. She died in Texas in 1903.

Evelyn Sibley Lampman

Evelyn Sibley Lampman was born in Dallas, Oregon, which is a small town in Willamette Valley, mecca of the covered wagon pioneers. Her great-grandparents made that trip themselves. Her father was a lawyer which, in a small town, meant he served various terms as mayor, district attorney, and county judge. He was also a good storyteller and some of Evelyn's happiest recollections are of sitting around the fireplace, cracking walnuts (including one for the cat, who was fond of them), and taking turns reading aloud. Then her father would

179

tell her stories, often of the early settlers of the Willamette Valley and of the Indians on the reservation twenty miles away. Her father was very sympathetic with the Indians and their problems, a rare thing in those days, and when they came to town they always stopped by to see him. Through his stories, her father was able to make many of these settlers and the Indians of that time, whom Evelyn never saw, very real to her.

After completing her schooling locally, Evelyn went on to Oregon State and was graduated from there, with a degree in Education. However, instead of teaching, she took a job in a Portland radio station as a continuity writer. In addition, she gave a daily cooking talk over the air.

Marriage followed and two daughters, which occupied Evelyn full time. With her husband's death eight years later, she went back to radio work as continuity chief, which led to her appointment as Educational Director of special programs that were being broadcast into the classrooms of the Portland Public Schools. She wrote all the programs herself. Her first book for children was published in 1948 and, in time, she was able to give up her radio work and concentrate entirely on her books, as she had done ever since.

Until the end of 1972, Mrs. Lampman lived in the same house she and her husband had bought thirty years before. It was big, old and drafty, with dark paneling and high ceilings. There were nine rooms and a huge yard, gradually growing into a jungle—and Evelyn loved it. Prodded by friends and family, she finally sold it and moved to a new house in an apple orchard on the outskirts of Portland, which, she says, "in time will begin to feel like home." Among her many published books are *Rattlesnake Cave, Go Up The Road, Cayuse Courage,* and *The Year of Small Shadow.*